"Our Passion Will Never Die,"

Demetrio said intensely. "We may hate each other, but we can't stop wanting each other. That will be true as long as we live."

"It may be true for you," Reva said coldly, "but not for me."

He paled. "You're lying."

"If that's what you want to believe."

He'd gotten close to her, so that she had to look up into his face. She met his eyes, hoping he couldn't tell her heart was beginning to beat strongly. She could sense the warmth from his body with its subtle scent of earth and arousal. It had always been a powerful erotic enticement, drawing her to him from the first moment.

"Look at me, Reva," he commanded quietly, "and tell me again that our passion is dead."

Dear Reader,

You know, there are some months here at Silhouette Desire that I feel are simply perfect! Naturally, I think each and every Desire book is just wonderful, but occasionally the entire lineup is so special I have to mention each book separately.

Let's start with *Hazards of the Heart* by Dixie Browning. This talented author has been writing for the line since nearly the very beginning—over ten years ago! Still, it's hard for me to believe that this is her *fiftieth* Silhouette book. *Hazards of the Heart* is highlighted as our *Man of the Month,* and it also contains a special letter from Dixie to you, her loyal readers.

Joan Johnston is fast becoming a favorite, but if you haven't yet experienced her sexy western-flavored stories, please give her a try! *The Rancher and the Runaway Bride* is the first of her new series, *Hawk's Way,* which takes place—mostly—on a Texas ranch. The stories concern the lives—and new loves—of the two Whitelaw brothers and their sassy sister.

A book from Lass Small is always a delight, and this time around we have *A Disruptive Influence.* What—or *who?*—is this disruptive influence? Why, read and find out.

As far as I'm concerned, Nancy Martin has been too long from the list, therefore I'm *thrilled* with *Good Golly, Miss Molly.* Doreen Owens Malek is another author we just don't see enough of, so I'm equally excited about *The Harder They Fall.* And I love Lucy Gordon's emotional writing style. If you're also a fan, don't miss *Married in Haste.*

Six spectacular books by six dynamite authors. Can you ask for anything more?

Until next month, happy reading!

Lucia Macro
Senior Editor

LUCY GORDON
MARRIED IN HASTE

SILHOUETTE *Desire*®

Published by Silhouette Books New York

America's Publisher of Contemporary Romance

SILHOUETTE BOOKS
300 East 42nd St., New York, N.Y. 10017

MARRIED IN HASTE

Copyright © 1993 by Lucy Gordon

ISBN: 0-373-05777-6

First Silhouette Books printing April 1993

Printed in the U.S.A.

LUCY GORDON

met her husband-to-be in Venice, fell in love the first evening and got engaged two days later. They're still happily married and now live in England with their three dogs. For twelve years Lucy was a writer for an English women's magazine. She interviewed many of the world's most interesting men, including Warren Beatty, Richard Chamberlain, Roger Moore, Sir Alec Guinness and Sir John Gielgud.

In 1985 she won the *Romantic Times* Reviewers' Choice Award for Outstanding Series Romance Author. She has also won a Golden Leaf Award from the New Jersey Chapter of the RWA, was a finalist for the RWA Golden Medallion in 1988 and won the 1990 Rita Award in the Best Traditional Romance category for *Song of the Lorelei*.

One

___

The clock on Demetrio Corelli's desk said it was one in the morning. He glanced at it, then at the silent telephone, and rose impatiently to go and stand by the window.

He was on the thirty-fifth floor, and from here he had a good view of his city. He thought of Milan as *his* city partly because he owned a good deal of it—far more than the public records showed—but mostly because he had made it his, through fighting, scheming, and hard, slogging work. At thirty-eight he was a multimillionaire, master of a vast industrial empire that he had built from nothing. His inflexible will and uncompromising business methods had made him a fearful legend. What he wanted, he took—quickly if he could, patiently if he must.

Once he had thought he'd found the perfect woman, the perfect love. He'd moved fast to claim her, only to find that love had turned to ashes. She was gone, but the matter wasn't over. Nothing was ever over until it was settled to his satisfaction. His enemies said, "Demetrio never sleeps," and when they said it they shivered.

They would have shivered now if they could have seen the look in his eyes. He was about to take the biggest gamble of his life, and he was determined to win. Nothing was going to stand in his way, not even the wishes of the woman he'd once loved.

The telephone rang. He crossed the huge office in two strides to snatch up the receiver. "Yes?" he snapped.

A man spoke. "She's boarded the plane. I'm just about to follow."

"Be careful," Demetrio growled. "Keep her in your sight, but don't let her notice you, whatever you do."

As the London-to-Milan flight took off, Reva Horden wondered for the hundredth time whether she was wise to accept this assignment.

It was the first time in her ten years as a photojournalist that she'd ever asked herself such a question. She'd always preferred her jobs to be dramatic, even dangerous. To Reva, a challenge was like a red rag to a bull, and the crazier it was, the better she liked it. It was an attitude that had cost her dearly. Because of it, she had been wounded, chased and threatened. Because of it, she had lost her love.

Her jaw set as she thought of Demetrio Corelli. She hadn't seen him for a year, but just the hint of his name could bring all the old antagonism and hostility bubbling up inside her as if it were yesterday. No other man had ever made her so angry. And no other man had ever had the same power to arouse her body with a word or a look.

When she'd heard that *Domani,* the Italian newsmagazine, wanted her for a difficult assignment, she'd instinctively jumped at the chance to work for one of the world's most prestigious publications. But the next thought had been "It means going to Milan."

Milan, where she'd met Demetrio Corelli and immediately wanted him with such burning, insane desire that she'd mistaken it for love; Milan, where Demetrio had proposed after a whirlwind week, where they'd married and lived in a blissful erotic paradise, until reality intruded and she realized that her husband was a monster of stubborn selfishness; Milan, where Demetrio still lived, where he'd tried to imprison her, locking her in her room as some nineteenth-century husband might have. But he'd been misled by her slender, graceful form, and he'd forgotten that she had the strength of an athlete. She'd escaped by climbing through the window onto a tree, but the memory of it still made her burn with outrage.

Demetrio's behavior had been so infamous that she'd sworn never to see or speak to him again. She'd braced herself for an onslaught of demands for her to return, but there had been no demands. His secretary had sent her clothes after her to England. From Demetrio himself there had been a deadly silence. She told herself she was glad. It would make it easier to stick to her resolve not to think of him.

She realized that she was thinking of him now, and gave herself a little shake. She was being absurd. Milan was a big place. He would never know she was there.

When the next call came, Demetrio was sitting impatiently by the phone.

"I'm at Milan airport," said the same man who had called before. "We've landed. She's collecting her baggage."

"I have a car waiting for her," Demetrio said. "Call me when she's in it."

He replaced the phone and went once more to stand by the window. But this time he was looking into the distance, where the first streaks of dawn were beginning to appear, and his eyes were hard.

Reva yawned as she emerged from customs. The flight had left her stiff and tired, and she was longing for a shower and a coffee. The editor had promised that a chauffeur would meet her plane, and to her relief a man carrying a placard with *Domani* written on it was waiting for her.

"Buon giorno, Signora Corelli," he said.

"Signorina Horden," she replied.

"I am here to drive you to the Hotel Palazzo. Let me take your bags."

She relinquished the trolley piled high with her luggage and her precious equipment and followed him out of the airport to the waiting car. He loaded her bags into the trunk while Reva slid into the back seat, yawning again, and indulging in the luxury of stretching out her long legs, which had been cramped on the aircraft. She glanced at the driver as he went to park the trolley and almost immediately collided with a middle-aged man. Reva recognized him as someone she'd seen on the plane. She watched sleepily as he turned away and went into a telephone booth. Then the car started to move, and he vanished from sight.

The dawn was well advanced now, bathing everything in a soft gray light. She recognized the long, straight lines of the Via Boccaccio, and memories flooded back to her, memories of the first time she'd seen this street. . . .

She'd been after a corrupt British politician who had disappeared, leaving many innocent people ruined. He'd been presumed dead, but Reva had tracked him to Milan and dogged his footsteps, determined to get a clear shot that would establish his identity. Thinking only of her work, she'd darted across the Via Boccaccio without looking either way. The next moment there had been a squeal of brakes and she'd been sprawling on the ground, staring into the radiator of a Rolls-Royce.

A man leapt out and leaned down to take hold of her. "Are you hurt?" he asked sharply in Italian.

Reva barely heard him. Looking around frantically, she saw her prey vanishing into the crowd. "Let me go," she said in English, struggling as he helped her to her feet.

"Not until I'm sure you're all right," he responded in fluent English, keeping hold of her.

"I'm all right, I'm fine. *Let me go.*"

"Just a minute," he said firmly. "I don't want you 'discovering' injuries later and bringing an action against me—"

"I'll bring an action against you, all right," she snapped. "For hindering me from doing my job. Oh, for heaven's sake! He's gone now. It's too late."

She had to raise her voice for the last words, because the air was split by the sound of irate motorists yelling and blaring their horns. She'd managed to bring one side of the Via Boccaccio to a standstill, and everywhere she could see waving fists.

"*Signorina . . .*" A policeman appeared. He was scowling at the chaos she had created, but his manner became instantly respectful when he recognized the man. "Signor Corelli—"

Corelli answered smoothly. Reva couldn't understand the words, but she recognized in him a natural authority that would be the same in any language. He finished by drawing her toward his car and urging her firmly into the back seat. "Look here," she said furiously, "I'm not—"

"Shut up and get in," he muttered. "Do you want to be arrested?" He slammed the door shut and rapped out an order to the driver, and the car started moving. Even through her annoyance, Reva was alert enough to notice how the policeman cleared the way for them. But mostly she was consumed by indignation.

"Do you realize what you've done?" she demanded.

"The accident was your own fault," he said abruptly. "If you will go flying across roads without looking where you're going, you must expect to collide with traffic. You're not badly hurt if you've got enough breath to abuse me. However, I'm prepared to pay you a reasonable sum in return for your signature on a document renouncing all further claim—"

She exploded. "You have the most unspeakable gall of any man I've ever met!"

"Let's just say that I've met this situation before, and I'm well prepared."

"You mean you often run people down?" she inquired acidly.

"I've had women appear in front of my car without warning. They know who I am, and they've calculated what they can get."

"Then they have an advantage over me," Reva snapped. "Just who are you?"

Instead of answering, Corelli drew a sharp breath. Following his gaze, Reva saw what he had seen—the reflection of his chauffeur's grin in the rear-view mirror. He leaned forward and slammed the dividing glass shut.

For the first time, her head cleared enough for her to take in a few details. He was in his late thirties, with black hair, a lean, tanned face, and dark eyes. His well-shaped mouth was firm almost to the point of hardness, and the set of his chin spoke of resolution. Authority radiated from every line of his long, taut frame, which was sheathed in a suit of superb cut that Reva guessed had cost a fortune.

Most women would have found him powerfully attractive, but she was too cross. "In any case, you can keep your money," she said. "It wouldn't compensate me for the damage you've done."

His dark eyes gleamed with irony. "Very clever, but I doubt if you can think of a trick to hoist up the price that I haven't come across before. Just what would 'compensate for the damage I've done'?"

"Tell me where I can find Michael Denton," Reva said emphatically.

She had the satisfaction of seeing that he was taken aback. "Just who is Michael—?"

"He's a British member of parliament who vanished off a beach last month, leaving behind a pile of clothes and a lot of unanswered questions. Only he didn't drown. He's here in Milan, and I had him in my sights when you knocked me over."

His eyes narrowed. "What are you, a detective?"

"No, I'm a photojournalist, and you've just robbed me of the scoop of the decade."

"You persist in regarding me as responsible for everything," he retorted angrily. "But if you'd watched the traffic—"

"If I'd watched the traffic, I'd have lost him."

"Well, you've lost him anyway."

"I know," she cried in anguish.

He shrugged in a way that infuriated her. "So what does it matter? There will be other scoops."

"Of course it matters. It's my job. It's important to me to do it well. Could you do your job if you shrugged and said it didn't matter?"

"That's different."

"No, it isn't. I don't know what your work is, except that it seems to make you remarkably conceited. But I'll bet you take a pride in it, don't you?"

"Yes," he said slowly. "Yes, I do."

"So do I. Now I've got to start all over again, thanks to you." Suddenly she noticed her surroundings through the window, and she pushed back the dividing glass. "I'll get out here," she told the chauffeur.

But the car didn't even slow down. "Why here?" Corelli asked her.

"Because we've just passed the Garibaldi Hotel, where I'm staying."

"Stop," Corelli ordered, and they came to a halt. "Giorgio is very well trained," he explained, with the hint of an apologetic smile. "He takes his orders only from me."

Reva got out, seething again at the certainty that this insufferable man was making fun of her. But before she could put her indignation into words, he had closed the door, signaled to the chauffeur and moved off.

That had been their first meeting. In retrospect it seemed typical that it had been a fight. When she looked back over their short marriage, two things stood out: the quarrels, and the blazing, heart-stopping passion, which had been even stronger than the hostility—for a while.

Once in her room at the Hotel Garibaldi, she'd discovered she was more bruised and shaken than she'd realized. But the real injury was to be robbed of her prey. She tried to plan her next move, but her mind had some difficulty functioning. Corelli had made his way inside it and refused to leave. She'd been too angry to notice the feel of his hands as he raised her and urged her into the car, but her flesh seemed to have absorbed the imprint, and she could feel his touch now, with a disturbing intensity. She had a shower and lay down, trying to dismiss the sensation that something momentous had occurred in her life.

After an hour, there was a knock at her door and a note was delivered.

It read: Michael Denton will dine tonight at a trattoria on the edge of town. I shall collect you at eight o'clock and take you there. Demetrio Corelli.

Reva drew in her breath. An hour ago he hadn't even heard of Michael Denton. Now he knew where he dined, and when. This was a man with eyes that saw everywhere. It wasn't lost on her that he'd withheld the trattoria's name, thus preventing her going without him. But she was too excited to mind much about that, or about his high-handed tone.

At eight o'clock she descended to the lobby, neatly but casually dressed in sweater and slacks. She looked around for Corelli, but could see only a man in jeans and a short-sleeved shirt, leaning on the desk. She noticed his arms, brown and powerful, with curling black hairs, the broad muscular back and the narrow hips. Then, as she started to look around for her escort, the man turned, and she started as she recognized Corelli. The casual attire transformed him, and he looked younger. The full force of his masculine attraction came surging up to meet her, making her clutch the rail as she fought off a moment's dizziness. "I've come to make amends," he said with a smile.

The smile almost made her dizzy again. He had a charm that was as forceful as everything else about him. She discovered that in the evening that followed. There was no chauffeur tonight. He drove her to the trattoria himself. Michael Denton wasn't there, but he promised her he would come. When she asked how he could be so sure, he smiled and said, "I have a lot of friends."

Soon she forgot even Michael Denton, as the magic of the evening began to weave a spell about her. Demetrio's sheer, blazing masculine vitality scorched her. His eyes were fixed on her with an intensity that told her he was mentally undressing her. She knew she ought to be outraged at this blatant sexism, but how could she be? She was mentally undressing *him*.

Before the evening was half-over, she knew she wanted him, shamelessly and with a need that dwarfed anything that had gone before in her life. It was almost frightening to desire a man that much. But his own desire, reaching out to her, was a reassurance.

But she wasn't so overwhelmed that she failed to notice when Michael Denton appeared and took a seat a few tables away. Demetrio leaned forward to whisper in her ear, his lips brushing against her skin in a way that made tremors go through her. "He's living here as Harold Acres," he murmured. "I have here a complete dossier on him. I meant to give it to you earlier but . . . I forgot."

She forced herself to subdue her physical excitement and read the dossier. After only a few sentences, she knew it was pure gold, and from then on her whole being was concentrated on it. Everything was there, even the numbers of the Swiss bank accounts in which Denton had stored loot stolen from a collapsed company. Quietly she rose and stood a little way off, among some trees. From her bag she produced a small camera and took shot after shot. Then she crept back to the table.

"Now can we get back to what we were talking about?" Demetrio asked, laying his hand over hers.

"No, I have to send this film off to England," she said, gathering her things together. "There's no time to lose."

With a sigh of resignation, he went with her to the car. On the journey back he made a call on the car phone. When it was over, he said, "A courier is waiting for us at my office. He'll take your film to England tonight."

Sure enough, a man was there at the office. She gave him the film and an address, and he promised to deliver it direct from the airport.

"Now…" Demetrio murmured when they were alone.

"Now I need somewhere to work," she said.

He stopped dead in the act of opening his arms. "But you've done your work."

"Not completely. I have to knock out a story with all those details you gave me."

"But you're a photographer. Can't someone else do that?" he demanded, clearly outraged.

"Do you really think I'm going to let another journalist in on this? I can do text if I set my mind to it, and I've set my mind to it."

"Maria Vergine!" he shouted. But he controlled himself at once. "All right. You can use my office."

In his office, she went through the dossier, making furious notes. Then she used his computer to dash out the story. At first light, she made a call: "Night editor, please. Hello, Bill? I've found Denton. There's a film on its way, and I'll fax some text to you in a minute. It's a scorcher. Names, bank accounts, the lot. Bye."

"Did he get a word in edgeways?" Demetrio asked wryly. He'd been sitting in silence, watching her.

"I don't think so. Why, does it matter? I'm doing the work. All he has to do is listen. How does your fax machine work? No, it's okay. Don't tell me. I know this make."

"How fortunate." It was only much later that she recalled the edge in his voice. She was caught up in the grip of professional euphoria, oblivious to the fact that he didn't share her excitement.

"My first really big scoop," she said exultantly, "and a lot of it's due to you. Don't worry. I'll make sure you get some sort of credit, but it'll be a small one, I'm afraid—"

He interrupted her sharply. "I absolutely forbid you to mention my name in any connection with this business. Are you mad? Do you think I want 'credit' from your little rag?"

The scornful way he said "little rag" annoyed her. "A newspaper that sells over four million is hardly a little rag," she said coolly.

"A little rag exposing little scandals about little crooks," he repeated. "Nothing to get excited about."

"You can hardly call Denton a little crook."

"He is to me."

"Then why did you help me?"

"To please you. Your moment of glory seemed to mean so much to you."

"Why, you patronizing—" Reva choked off her words, remembering that she still needed to use his machine.

He grinned in a way that made her heart turn over even as she seethed. "Yes, it wouldn't do to insult me before you've sent the story through, would it?'' he said teasingly.

"I'll do it now," she said with dignity.

When she finished, she found him regarding her with a quizzical look on his face. His lips were just touched by a smile, and his eyes were inviting. Suddenly her annoyance drained away, to be replaced by tingling warmth. Why, she wondered, had she been wasting her time on Denton, when what she really wanted was to be in this man's arms—the very arms that were opening for her now? Dazed, she went into them.

The touch of his lips on hers was a searing revelation. Her whole body seemed to be going up in flames. No other kiss had ever evoked such a violent, instantaneous response, and for a moment she was stunned and shocked. Then she yielded to the sensations that were washing over her and began to kiss him back, urgently. Her mind was racing as hard as her pulse. Kissing alone could never be enough with this man. She wanted more, and he did, too. The pounding of his heart and the skilled movements of his hands and lips were telling her that with thrilling intensity.

The ringing of the telephone shattered her blissful dream.

Demetrio swore softly and snatched up the receiver. Reva clung to him, feeling faint from the strength of her response and from the ache of having it snatched away. As Demetrio listened, his expression, already impatient, became exasperated. "It's for you," he growled, holding it out to her. She took it with a shaking hand.

It was the night editor. "How did you know to call me here?'' she demanded raggedly. She didn't really care, but the question gave her time to gather her scattered wits.

"Your fax bore the Corelli marker," came Bill's voice. "All this stuff's very impressive, but is it for real?"

She was pulling herself together now, yielding to another sort of excitement, the professional kind that had always meant so much to her. "I got it from an impeccable source," she assured him.

"Well, as soon as the paper's gone to bed, I'll notify the police. They'll be on to the Italian police, so make sure you see the arrest."

"Right," she said, alert now. "I'll get out to his house straightaway."

"Fine. Stay in touch. And well done. After this, it's the top for you."

Reva replaced the phone and let out a cry of exultation. "I'm on my way. All I need now is to get pictures of the arrest. How can I get to his house?"

"It's a long way."

"But you could drive me out there, couldn't you?"

"I have a busy day—"

"Then lend me your chauffeur. Please, Demetrio—I'm so close...."

"Reva, look at me. What do you see?"

"I see you," she answered blankly.

"Yes, but what am I? Do you see me as a man with feelings and desires, or am I merely your courier, a faceless creature who turns up cars and information on demand? I've been wondering about it for the last couple of hours."

"I'm sorry," she said, instantly contrite. "I know I get carried away, but this is so important to me."

"I dare say," he responded through gritted teeth. "But when it's over—what then?"

"Then you'll have my eternal gratitude."

"I'd settle for your attention for five minutes," he growled.

She smiled at him. "You'll have all my attention. I promise."

He provided her with the car and the chauffeur. By midday Denton was in custody and she had a world exclusive. At midnight she was in Demetrio's arms again.

They made love in the little apartment attached to his office. The bed was single, but large enough for two people intent on uniting. Demetrio was a skilled lover, combining tenderness and vigor. Beneath the expensive suit, his body had the power and toughness of the manual worker he had once been. His broad chest and muscular thighs were legacies of the days when he'd worked on building sites to raise the money for a business course. Reva rejoiced in the beauty and strength of that body, trembling with delight at the feel of it against her and gasping with pleasure when he touched her intimately. His thrust into her had made her cry out in ecstasy.

Their sexual compatibility was a state of perfect bliss, and it was only later that she could see it as a trap. In those early days, they hardly ever had a real conversation because it was an effort not to touch each other all the time. Their lovemaking was glorious, heart-stopping, but it left no time for them to get to know each other as people. When she began to awaken from her happy dream, she had already been married six months to a man she was beginning to realize was still essentially a stranger. That was when their quarrels began.

Reva forced herself back to the present. She didn't want to remember any more. The blazing joy of the early months contrasted too cruelly with what had followed: the disillusion when Demetrio had proved himself a monster who would use every trick to clip her wings. In the end he'd even imprisoned her to stop her leaving the house. Reva's soul still burned with rage at the memory of Demetrio turning the key in the lock, ignoring her frantic hammering and her demands to be released. How could any man, in this day and age, think he had the right to control his wife by locking her up? But this man had thought so. He would have kept her a prisoner until he'd broken her spirit if she hadn't managed to escape.

All that was a year in the past, and since then she had regarded passion as dead and gone for her. Passion was an enemy, a betrayer. Her desire for Demetrio's marvelous body, with its subtle erotic skills, had led her into a terrible trap, but she had learned her lesson.

There were plenty of men available. Her large blue eyes, her warm skin and her abundance of deep honey-colored hair had always attracted them, but now there was something more. Her marriage had left her with the ripe, sensual beauty of a woman who has experienced complete physical fulfillment. The movements of her curved lips carried echoes of nights in Demetrio's arms, whispering words of desire and provocation. Men flocked around her like bees to a honey pot. But she wanted nothing to do with them. She'd made her decision, and she meant to stick to it. No more love. No more desire. Only work, and the satisfaction of her flowering career.

She heard the driver call, "Hotel Palazzo," and pulled herself together. She was brooding, and that was something she'd vowed not to do. The past was another life. She'd put it behind her, and Demetrio Corelli was no more than a bitter memory.

The hotel was an imposing establishment. She would have preferred something simpler, but *Domani* had made the arrangements. She followed the porter to the suite reserved for her, tipped him and kicked off her shoes.

There would be time later to unpack. For now all she wanted was a shower, so that when she met the editor of *Domani,* later that day, she would be alert. She stripped off her clothes and tossed them into the laundry basket in the bathroom. She secured her hair on top of her head and got into the shower. As the water streamed over her, she felt it wash the night away, and wished it could wash away her bitter memories as easily.

At last she stepped out, feeling better, and wrapped a bath towel around her. Now she would call room service and ask for some breakfast.

But on the threshold of the bedroom she stopped, frozen with shock and horror.

Demetrio Corelli was standing there, a look of triumph on his face.

Two

"*You,*" she breathed in disbelieving horror. "How did you get in here?" For answer, he held up a key. "You've got a key to my room?" she asked, aghast. "But how? Oh, I don't believe this! It must be a nightmare!"

"Indeed?" he inquired coldly. "When you got a summons to Milan, did you really not guess that I'd be here, waiting?"

"Of course not. If I'd dreamed I was going to meet you nothing on earth would have got me here. I told you in my last letter that I never wanted to see you again, and I meant it."

Demetrio regarded her cynically. "I see. Then it's just as well I was cautious enough to lie low until you'd arrived. It's a pleasure to see you again, dear wife."

"Well, it's not a pleasure for me," she snapped. "I want you to leave, *now.*"

Instead of answering, he continued to watch her, his head a little to one side, an inscrutable expression in his eyes. "You haven't changed a bit," he said at last. "Still the same hothead who never looks further ahead than five minutes."

"Yes, the worst decision of my life was made on the spur of the moment, wasn't it?" she said. "And I had plenty of time to regret it."

He shrugged. "We both regretted it. But with me impulsiveness was an aberration. With you it's a way of life. It made you delightfully unpredictable."

"I'll make a prediction now that you can count on," she told him, seething. "If you don't get out of my room this minute, I'll call the manager and have you thrown out."

He laughed. The sound unsettled Reva, but she wouldn't let him see that. "You think you're too important to be thrown out of a hotel, don't you?" she said coldly. "Well, you're wrong, and in another minute you're going to discover it."

She reached for the bedside telephone, but he got there first and held the receiver down with his hand. "For your own sake, don't try that," he said.

"For my own sake? Do you have the nerve to threaten me?"

"I wasn't—"

"That's just your style, isn't it? Bullying and threats. How well I remember it!"

For the first time his composure fractured. "You dare say that I bullied you? Have you forgotten so soon that I treated you like a queen—"

"Until the day the pretense bored you and you locked me up like a prisoner. I haven't forgotten that, and I never will, not until the day I die."

She thought she saw him grow a little paler. For a moment he said nothing, and Reva had the chance to study him. He was thinner, and his face was older. There were new lines about his dark eyes, which seemed slightly sunken beneath thick black brows, with shadows around them. His mouth was tense and looked as if it smiled less easily than before. He had the appearance of a man who often worked through the night with too little food.

But he was still the same man she remembered. Beneath the expensive suit, the lines of his long, hard body suggested strength and suppleness, just as in the past. And his hands has the same marvelous combination of power and grace.

The sight of those hands was almost her undoing. Memories of their skill flooded back to her. Demetrio knew how to touch a woman where it thrilled her most, how to prolong a caress with infinite subtlety, until her body was throbbing with need for deeper caresses and her heart pounded with excitement. There had been such beauty in his arms, and such disillusionment in the morning. It was all false. He'd used his sexual magic to try to make her his slave. And Reva was no man's slave.

Until then she'd been too startled and angry to think of her attire, but suddenly she realized how vulnerably naked she was beneath the towel. It was skimpy, covering her only from the swell of her breasts to the tops of her thighs. She thought desperately of her clothes, still packed up in locked bags on the far side of the room, with Demetrio standing between her and them. "Very well," she said in a tight voice, "if you want to talk, we'll talk—although I can't see what we have to say to each other."

"Two people who once loved each other should always be able to find something to say," he replied, looking at her steadily.

"I never loved you," she said emphatically.

"I think you're lying."

"Think what you like, but get out of my way so that I can find some clothes."

He glanced at the bags and stood aside. Reva quickly took the smaller one and opened it, pulling out some underwear and a pair of slacks. "Turn around," she ordered. "I'm not moving this towel in front of you."

"You weren't always so modest with me," he reminded her. There was a strange, wry look about his mouth that might have been pain.

She flung him a look of hate for recalling the days when she'd flaunted her beautiful nakedness before his hot, eager eyes, both of them yearning for the moment when he would seize her in his arms and blend her body with his own. There had been no thought of modesty then. But now...

"Turn away," she repeated.

He shrugged. "It makes very little difference, but to please you..." He turned his back.

Reva reached for the top of the towel, where it was tucked in, but stayed her hand. She was near the door. Once in the corridor, she could scream for help and have him ejected. Moving quietly, she took two steps nearer the door, then sprinted.

But he was there before her, moving with incredible speed, seizing her in both arms and holding her tight. "How lucky that I was watching the mirror," he said as she tried to struggle. "I guessed you weren't to be trusted."

"I don't have to be trustworthy to a man who behaves like you," she said through gritted teeth. "I don't owe you any honor." To her horror, the sensation of being pressed against him was sending a tingling pleasure through her body. Her mind's antagonism counted as nothing beside the memory of rapture hidden deep in her flesh.

"For heaven's sake, keep still and listen," he told her. "It wouldn't have done you any good to get out of that door. This is one hotel I can't be thrown out of. I happen to own it."

She drew a quick breath. "I might have guessed."

"Yes, you might. But, as I said, your total lack of calculation in everything you do has always been a disadvantage to you."

"Better to be that way than to go through life calculating every detail," she snapped.

A look of weariness seemed to come over his face, and his arms relaxed. "You always came off best in our fights," he said with a touch of bitterness.

"That's not what I remember."

"You have the gift of the wounding remark. Like a fool, I was gentleman enough to quarrel in your language, where you have the advantage."

She managed partly to free herself, but he kept hold of her wrist. "I just want to get my old clothes out of the bathroom," she said.

"And lock the door against me. No, thank you. I'm not going to shout through a locked door."

"All right, I promise not to."

"But you don't owe me any honor," he reminded her. "Thank you for the warning. I'll keep you here until I've had my say."

He released her, and she sat on the bed, pulling the towel around her again. Demetrio eyed her for a moment, then went quickly into the bathroom and emerged with another towel, which he tossed to her. She put it around her shoulders, hugging it across her breasts, and glared at him. "I suppose you knew I'd been hired by *Domani*?"

"For a woman who accuses me of calculating every move, you're remarkably slow-witted today," he said ironically. "You can do better than that."

She was briefly speechless while the implication sank in. "You arranged for me to be hired by *Domani*?" she asked at last, struggling for words.

"Of course. There was no other way of getting you here."

"You mean—?" As the monstrous truth dawned on her, she exploded. "You arranged *everything*, didn't you?"

"Every last detail," he confirmed quietly. "The editor of *Domani* owes me a favor, and he was glad to agree to my suggestion that he offer you work. I arranged your flight, your car, and, of course, your hotel. You were watched every step of the way. One of my men traveled on the plane with you and called me as soon as you got into the car. I was waiting across the street when you arrived here."

"I don't believe what I'm hearing," she said wildly. "How can any man be so devious? So you thought you could make me your prisoner again? You were wrong, Demetrio. Nothing on this earth will ever make me come back to you."

"Have I asked you to come back to me?" he demanded coldly.

"No, of course not. Asking isn't your way, is it? You command, you set traps, and when your prey is caught off guard you slam the cage shut."

"Will you harp on forever about one incident?" he asked harshly. "Yes, I locked the door on you. If I hadn't, you might be dead now. You wanted to dash into the heart of a war zone where one photographer had already died, and I have this irrational objection to seeing my wife killed."

"Fine sentiments! The truth is that you'd laid down the law and you expected to be obeyed. Other husbands don't make prisoners of their wives."

"Other husbands don't have to cope with wives who rush off to danger without a backward glance."

"I warned you about my career. You said you knew. I didn't understand then that you'd say anything to get your own way and go back on it afterward."

"I never deceived you," he said harshly. "I respected your wish to work after our marriage, but I thought you meant reasonable work."

"Reasonable as *you* define it. Posed portraits, picturesque sunsets, advertising shots—all of them so appallingly, oppressively *safe*. No life, no excitement, no point. I'm an action photographer. I shoot life on the run."

"Yes, you always got your kicks from taking pictures that offended someone," he said dryly. "If there wasn't a 'heavy' trying to snatch your camera or club you over the head, you got bored."

"A news picture is one that someone, somewhere, wants to stop me from taking," she said, quoting her favorite editor. "And that's the business I'm in."

"And I was so foolish as to think you'd consider my feelings when we married," he said bitterly. "Well, if you learned your lesson, so did I, the day you wanted to abandon me for a war zone. What was I supposed to do? Say, 'Off you go, my dear, and if you survive, send me a postcard with a bullet hole through it'?''

"Was it my danger that troubled you," she asked, "or the thought of that business dinner I was going to miss? 'Nothing gets in the way of business.' *Your* motto. You didn't like it when I applied it to *my* business."

Demetrio sighed. "Let the past bury its dead, Reva. It's pointless to reopen old wounds."

"I agree. But then why am I here?"

"Because there is something I want you to do—not for me, but for Nicoletta."

At the mention of Demetrio's younger sister, Reva's face softened. Nicoletta had been eighteen when she'd seen her last, a black-eyed beauty with a zest for life and an impulsiveness that almost matched Reva's own. "How is she?" she asked eagerly. "Has she ever forgiven me?"

"Of course. Far from blaming you for deserting me, she's convinced the whole thing was my fault. The two of you should get on as well as ever."

"That's taking a lot for granted," Reva said quickly.

"You surely won't refuse to meet her. That would hurt her deeply. She's longing to tell you all about the young man she's fallen in love with."

"You told Nicoletta that I was coming here?" Reva said. "Did you also tell her how you manipulated me into coming?"

"Not . . . exactly," he admitted uncomfortably.

"No, because she's the most honest, straightforward soul alive, and your methods would shock her. What does she want me to do for her?"

"Help her to get married."

Reva looked up, frowning. "But I'd be terrible at all that bridal-bouquet stuff. Why, we—" She checked herself. This conversation was a minefield.

"We married as quickly and quietly as possible," Demetrio finished for her. "Thus giving offense to several hundred people who'd expected to be invited."

"It was a wedding, not a business convention."

"Anyway, that's not what I mean. If Nicoletta's wedding takes place, I shall confine myself to paying the bills. The actual arrangements will be made by the groom's family. The heir to Count Torvini will be married as the Torvinis have always been married, in the cathedral here in Milan, with a cardinal officiating."

"Count Torvini?" Reva echoed. She remembered the Torvinis, an ancient and distinguished family whose men tended to become government ministers or high-ranking church dignitaries. The women married into the aristocracy or politics, and every one of them was bristling with pride. "I met the count once at a reception we gave," she recalled.

"That's right."

"I don't think I liked him. He was too condescending, too aware of what a big favor he was doing us by deigning to set foot in our house."

Demetrio shrugged. "I meet that attitude all the time. It's no secret that I fought my way up from nowhere, and there are many families who'd like to turn up their noses at me. But they dare not. I have my finger in too many pies. So they meet me, in business and in their homes. They pretend to treat me as one of themselves, while behind my back they tell each other what a barbarian I am."

"And none of this troubles you?" Reva asked, looking at him curiously.

He shrugged. "The dogs bark, but the caravan moves on. Let them think what they like, as long as they pay my price."

Reva nodded, recognizing the Demetrio she knew. "So Count Torvini is going to pay your price to the extent of letting his heir marry Nicoletta?" she guessed.

"That depends on you," Demetrio said slowly.

"What—exactly—do you mean?"

"He isn't keen to see his son marry my sister, but he doesn't want to offend me by mentioning my background. So he's gone about it more subtly, dropping hints about 'the sanctity of family life.' To be fair to him, he honestly believes what he preaches. He's known as a model husband, and to him the fact that I'm living apart from my wife is almost as much of a blot as my obscure origins."

"That's medieval," Reva said.

He shrugged. "The Torvinis *are* medieval."

"Then why do you bother with them? I've heard you say that titles mean nothing, that a man's own achievements are all that matter."

"And I still believe it. But Nicoletta's happiness is at stake. For her sake, I'll do all I can to smooth the way to this marriage." He paused, as if hoping she would suggest something. When she stayed silent, he took a deep breath and said, "I want you to return to me for a short while—just long enough to kill the rumors. After the wedding, you can do what you like."

Reva stared at him. "You invented this complicated plot just to ask me this? I suppose it wouldn't occur to you to just pick up the phone and ask me?"

"You'd have hung up. I had to get you here by any means I could."

"Of course—I remember now, you always preferred fighting on your own ground. You said victory was more certain that way."

"I like to win."

"No, you don't 'like' to win. You *have* to win. It's the only thing that matters, and to hell with what it does to anyone else."

"I'm not a sentimental man. I don't pretend to be. I can't afford it."

"You always said that when you wanted to justify some particularly unscrupulous piece of dealing, but what you call sentimentality I call human feeling, and thinking about other people and *their* rights."

Demetrio gave a grim laugh. "I come from a tough school, and it taught me to be careful how I 'think about' other people. While I'm doing all this thinking, they're going to stab me in the back."

"So you stab first."

"I survive," he said harshly. "Interpret that any way you want. Hate me as much as you like. I don't care. But do this for Nicoletta."

Her mind was in a whirl. She instinctively shied away from the thought of returning to Demetrio, even on this basis. But she loved Nicoletta, who had welcomed her warmly and had always treated her as a sister. She thought of the beautiful dark-haired girl, with her generous heart and impish humor. Nicoletta would never hesitate to do a favor for someone she loved. Playing for time, Reva said, "How long would it be for?"

"A couple of months, perhaps three."

"Oh, no. I shall have a lot of work to do in the next three months."

"That's not what you told the editor of *Domani* when he asked you to keep the next three months clear," Demetrio said, surveying her wryly. "You said you would refuse all other bookings."

Reva glared at him, furious at the trap he'd set her, and how easily she'd fallen into it. "No doubt you told him to say that," she snapped.

"Of course. I had to make sure the ground was well prepared."

"But you overlooked something. If there's no work for me at *Domani* I'll have to take on other assignments to earn my living. I can't go three months without work."

"Then I'll pay you. It'll be a business deal."

He had an answer for everything, she thought. It was like the old days, when he'd always been able to make it sound so reasonable that she should do exactly what he wanted.

"I can't do it," she said firmly. "You may have forgotten how our marriage ended, but I never will."

"Forget?" he demanded harshly. "Do you think I shall ever forget how you made a fool of me in front of the whole of Milan?"

"If that's all you care about—"

"I have to care about it. It damages my business if I lose face."

"Business," she echoed bitterly. "Always business."

"It was business that dressed you in the best clothes money could buy."

"But I never wanted the best clothes money could buy, Demetrio. I only wanted to dress like myself. It was you who insisted on trying to turn me into someone else, getting your secretary to make me appointments with couture houses because that was how the wife of a big industrialist was expected to dress."

"Well, you *were* the wife of a big industrialist," he said impatiently.

"I was also myself—me, Reva. And I got scared, because I could see my real self being swallowed up."

"Do you have to make a tragedy just because I wanted you to dress well?" he demanded.

"The tragedy is that you don't understand what it was that upset me. You didn't then, you don't now, and you never will. Our minds never met, not for one moment. That's why we always quarreled."

"What does it matter that we quarreled? We always resolved our differences satisfactorily in bed."

"Not satisfactorily," she said at once. "The differences were always there afterward. Passion solves nothing. Now that my passion for you is dead, I can see that clearly."

"I don't believe you," he said simply. "Our passion will never die. We may hate each other, but we can't stop wanting each other. That will be true as long as we live."

There was an intense note in his voice that might have been sincerity, but Reva heard in it only the old desire to control her, and she resisted it with all her strength. She was no longer Demetrio Corelli's dupe. "It may be true for you," she said coldly, "but not for me."

He paled. "You're lying."

"If that's what you want to believe."

He'd gotten close to her, and she had to look up to see into his face. She wanted to escape, to get out of the circle of his dangerous spell, but that would be an admission. The moment she moved he would know she feared to be near him. So she forced herself to stay where she was, head high, meeting his eyes, hoping he couldn't tell that her heart was beginning to beat strongly. She could sense the warmth from his body, with its subtle scent of earth and arousal. How well she remembered it, with its suggestion of hot, dark fertility, searing rapture, and ecstatic release. It had always been a powerful erotic enticement, drawing her to him from the first moment, making her blind and deaf to all warnings about his true nature.

"Look at me, Reva," he commanded quietly, "and tell me again that our passion is dead."

Something was making it difficult to speak. "Stop this, Demetrio," she choked out.

"Why should I stop it? If you really feel nothing, you have no reason to care what I do. Tell me it's all over, that your body no longer responds to me. It's easy to say that—isn't it? *Isn't it?*"

Looking into his eyes, she saw a smouldering heat that touched off fires deep within her. The walls she'd built so high and strong around her began to crumble. She tried to back away, but he took her shoulders and drew her nearer. "Say it, Reva. Say that your heart stays cold and steady when you're close to me. Say that you don't remember how it felt to be in my arms . . . to have me inside you . . . loving you. . . ."

Her lips tried to frame the words, but no sound came out. Her heart was thundering madly. She meant to push him away, but she couldn't move as he drew her closer and closer, until she was pressed against him. She had no choice but to look up as his mouth descended purposefully on hers.

The moment their lips touched, the past year vanished. All the safe indifference she'd striven to create was revealed as a futile delusion. This was the man who had once brought her sleeping body to life, and that memory would never die. He could rekindle it with the lightest caress of his mouth. But she wouldn't give him the satisfaction of knowing it. She held herself still while he left her mouth and began to trail kisses down her long neck.

"Say it, Reva," he repeated. "Say this means nothing to you."

"Nothing," she said, hearing the word come out as a gasp. "Let me go, Demetrio. Admit defeat."

"That's one thing I never admit," he growled. He cupped her face between his hands and renewed the assault on her mouth, his lips moving in a way that was half promise, half threat. She fought him in desperate silence, refusing to part her lips as he was urging, for if she did that she would be lost.

But she couldn't refuse to feel what his kiss was doing to her. Bittersweet, familiar sensations had awoken and were insidiously possessing her flesh, defying her frantic attempts to ignore them. Warmth began in her loins and radiated outward, making the soft inner surfaces of her thighs sensitive and eager for the feel of him there. Demetrio had always been able to arouse her quickly, but now it was happening at lightning speed, helped along by a thousand memories.

He was easing his tongue between her lips and she no longer had the strength—or perhaps it was the will—to prevent him. Shudders went through her as he caressed the inside of her mouth with a skill that scared her. Her very bones seemed to be melting. She couldn't even protest when he took hold of the flimsy towel and pulled it away. She knew this was madness, but she was back in the old, ecstatic dream, where nothing mattered but to be in this man's arms.

Her heart was beating madly as Demetrio lifted her in his arms and carried her toward the bed. As he laid her down, she opened her arms helplessly to him. He dropped his head to enclose one hard-peaked nipple between his lips, and a soft moan broke from her. She was doing everything she'd sworn not to do, yielding like an

inexperienced girl, but she couldn't help it. Her mind
might reject this man, but her body wanted him with all
the intensity of long deprivation.

She felt a light touch on her thighs and opened them
for him. His fingertips were tracing the old, familiar
pattern on the delicate inner skin, and it was driving her
crazy, as it had always done. She dug her fingernails into
his back as the touch moved slowly higher, willing him
on. When he softly touched the heart of her sensuality,
she trembled, and the next instant she was tearing open
the buttons on the front of his shirt and slipping her
hands inside. She was possessed by desire, by hurrying
eagerness to sink deeper into the blissful erotic dream into
which only he could take her. Let the world go by without her, as long as she had Demetrio's love.

Love! The little word had the magic power to set off
warning bells. They rang loud enough to pierce the fog of
delight that he was evoking in her with the old skill. The
cynical skill. The skill of a man who could perfect any
ability to gain his own ends. Love played no part in what
he was doing at this moment. She knew that, and had
stupidly allowed herself to forget it.

She began to struggle. "Let me go," she said breath-
lessly.

"No," he murmured against her flesh. "You don't really want me to let you go."

His assurance was another brand on the fire of alarm
that was sweeping away her desire. He was so sure he
could make her want what suited him. "Let me go," she
cried wildly.

"Be silent," he whispered as he kissed the sensitive skin
beneath her ear. "Don't fight me, Reva . . . Yield . . ."

Terrified, she put out a final, despairing effort and
fought him madly. *"No,"* she said violently. "Get away

from me, Demetrio. I mean that. Get away now and
don't ever touch me again.''

For a moment she thought he would refuse, but something he saw in her wild, desperate face seemed to strike
him like a blow. He moved blindly away from the bed,
stumbling slightly as he found his feet. Reva seized the
towel and pulled it around her naked body. At this moment, she hated her husband.

"You had to do that, didn't you?" she said bitterly.
"You had to conquer the 'little woman' to show how
powerful you are."

"Am I powerful?" he asked quietly. "It doesn't seem
so to me."

Reva barely heard him. "I want you to go, right now.
Our marriage is over. I'm sorry for Nicoletta, but even
for her I won't risk coming back, even briefly, to a man
who's so totally unscrupulous."

To her surprise, Demetrio made no further attempt to
argue. He left the room without giving her another look.
The moment the door was closed, she sprang up and ran
to it, slamming the bolt home. He wouldn't get in again.

She hurried back into the bathroom and got back into
the shower. As the water laved over her, she tried to believe it was washing away the touch of his hands and lips,
but at last she gave up. It wasn't Demetrio's touch she
was trying to obliterate, but her own response. After a
year apart, when she'd thought the old passion safely
dead, he'd brought it back to life with an ease that was
terrifying. At his lightest touch, her body had gone up in
flames. Now it ached for the fulfillment that had been so
close before being cruelly snatched away. His battle to
control her had almost ended in victory. And he knew it.
He must never be allowed to come so close again. She

must escape Milan today, before he had time to regroup his forces.

She tore open one of her bags and took out some fresh clothes, throwing them on any which way in her eagerness to be finished. When she was dressed, she fastened the bag again, checked her passport and money and prepared to leave. But as she reached out to lift the bag, there was a tap on the door.

She hesitated. It might be Demetrio, but she didn't think so. The tap had been too light and gentle. "Who is it?" she called.

"It's me, Nicoletta," came the reply.

Reva groaned inwardly. Of course Demetrio had one last trick up his sleeve. He'd sent his sister to plead with her. This would be the hardest moment to get through, but she would stay resolute and hope Nicoletta would forgive her. She opened the door.

At once she was enveloped by a whirlwind. Nicoletta's arms were about her neck, and Nicoletta's voice was in her ear, saying unbelievable things.

"Grazie, grazie," she cried. *"Mia sorella* . . . my sister. Always I have wished that you were really my sister, but now I feel you are, because of what you are doing for me."

The first twinges of alarm were beginning to niggle at Reva. "Nicoletta, please—"

The girl drew back from the bear hug in which she had wrapped Reva. Her beautiful young face was shining. "Don't say it," she commanded, laying a finger over Reva's mouth. "Don't tell me not to thank you. My heart is so full of love and gratitude for you."

The alarm was growing fast now. "What—what has Demetrio told you?" she asked uneasily.

"He has told me everything—how kind you are, how generously you agreed at once to help me. Oh, Reva, I have so much to tell you. I was so miserable, because if I cannot marry Guido I will simply die. But then my brother says you are coming to our rescue and I am so filled with happiness."

There was no doubt of her happiness. She was possessed by it, aglow with it, rays of joy beaming from her huge, dark eyes. And Demetrio was challenging Reva to crush that joy. Surely, she thought frantically, even Demetrio wouldn't dare do something so monstrous?

But he was there, standing in the doorway, watching his scheme unfold with sardonic eyes. Over Nicoletta's shoulder, Reva glared at him, silently mouthing the words, "I will never forgive you for this."

"You must come home with us now," Nicoletta said. "Everything is ready for you."

"You knew I was coming, then?" Reva said wryly.

"Of course I knew. Demetrio said you wouldn't refuse, because you are good and kind. He said there was no more generous person in the world than you. And I know he is right."

She was urging Reva toward the door as she spoke. "Why don't you go down ahead?" Reva said. "I want a word with Demetrio first."

Nicoletta kissed her cheek and departed, singing. The other two looked at each other in silence.

"I won't waste time with my opinion of your morals or your methods," she said at last. "It would be like water off a duck's back. I'll simply say this. I want your promise that you'll never touch me again, never enter my bedroom. If you should ever try—the deal's off."

"You have my word," Demetrio said at once. "Don't worry, Reva. My sister's happiness means too much for me to jeopardize it. Now, shall we go downstairs and let the world see what a happy, united couple we are?"

Three

When she reached the street, Reva saw Nicoletta streaking away in her little red sports car, leaving her no choice but to travel with Demetrio. He had dismissed his chauffeur for the day, and she found herself alone with him. He stopped her when she tried to get into the back seat. "Sit beside me," he said. "We still have things to talk about."

They sat in silence until they were well on their way out of the city. Then Reva said, "I'll come back and put a good face on it for Nicoletta's sake, but I want another bedroom. I won't go back to that room you locked me in."

"Of course not," Demetrio said, shrugging. "I don't live in that house anymore. I sold it months ago."

"But you loved that place. You used to call it the house you'd built from nothing."

He shrugged. "There were too many memories of you. I preferred to be completely rid of you."

After a brief silence, Reva said quietly, "I see."

"The new house is a few miles out of the city."

"What's it like?"

"Wait and you'll see."

Soon the car swung through a large wrought-iron gate. A hundred yards farther along, a house came into view. Reva gasped. "It's quite impressive, isn't it?" Demetrio agreed.

"It's massive. Why... it's a palace."

"The Palazzo Corsevo."

"That sounds familiar. Wait— I've heard you mention it."

"My mother worked here. When I was a child I used to run errands for the *padrone,* Baron Alessi."

"And now you own it," she said dryly. "Of course."

"May I ask what you mean by 'of course'?"

"It was only a matter of time before you yourself became the *padrone* where your family had been servants. I'm surprised it took you so long."

He didn't reply, and after a moment she glanced at him. His profile was as impassive as marble.

As they neared the house, Reva saw that it looked shabby and run-down. "It needs a lot of work," Demetrio said. "It was going to rack and ruin before I took it over. Any minute now, you'll meet Francesca. She's my new housekeeper. Ginetta, whom you knew, retired."

"What does Francesca know?"

"Officially, nothing. Your return today will be a wonderful surprise to us all. Unofficially, of course, all the servants understand why the mistress's room has been prepared."

"Do they realize I'm only here for a short time?"

"Of course not. If too many people know a secret, it gets out, and we can't afford a lot of gossip. We've buried our differences and had a grand reconciliation."

His dry, ironic tone enabled her to say, "How delightful for us."

At first she wasn't attracted to the huge neoclassical building, whose outside was forbidding. But inside it seemed to shrink and become cozier, and the flowers massed everywhere gave it a pleasant aspect. Francesca, who had evidently been briefed by Nicoletta, came forward to say, "Welcome to your new home, Signora Corelli. I hope you will be very happy here."

Reva said what was proper, and allowed an eager Nicoletta to conduct her to her room, under the curious eyes of the servants, all of whom seemed to have discovered some urgent task to perform in the great hall. Reva was burningly aware of their fascinated glances as she climbed the stairs, and she breathed a sigh of relief as soon as the door of her bedroom was firmly shut behind her.

"I prepared your room myself," Nicoletta said, smiling.

Here, too, there were flowers, and sunlight streamed in through the two floor-length windows. Reva had been ready to be polite, but it wasn't necessary. The room was charming in a traditional style, with a polished wood floor and a cream-and-gold decor that looked slightly shabby. Reva could see that it must once have been a gorgeous place. Now its air of faded grandeur gave it a gentle charm.

In the center of one wall was a double bed, that looked as if it could actually sleep four. The thought gave Reva a nasty jolt for a moment, but then she recalled that Italian beds tended to be massive, especially old ones. She remembered something else about Italian beds, too, and gingerly sat on the edge. Nicoletta laughed.

"I had a new mattress put on it for you," she said. "Modern and well sprung." She sat beside Reva and suddenly threw her arms around her. "My dear sister," she exclaimed joyfully, "I have so wanted to have you back. Home was terrible after you left. Demetrio was so fierce that no one dared to speak to him, even me. Now that you're home, everything will be all right."

"But I'm not home," Reva said hastily. "At least, not for good. This is just for you. Nothing has really changed between Demetrio and me."

"I understand, but—I remember when you married my brother. How I envied you. I thought it must be so marvelous to be in love as you two were."

"Were we?" Reva murmured wryly. "I wonder."

"Of course you were. Anybody could have seen it. It shone from you both. You couldn't bear to be apart for one moment. Surely you can't have forgotten?"

"Yes," Reva said slowly. "I had forgotten. So many other things have happened since."

"But when people love each other like that, it must be for ever," Nicoletta said earnestly. "I was sure of it then, but even more so now that I have a love of my own. I know that I shall love my Guido forever and ever and ever."

"Tell me about him," Reva said, glad to be able to turn the conversation. "Is he very handsome?"

"Oh, bellissimo," Nicoletta said joyously. "As soon as I see him I think he is beautiful like a god. And he is so charming and so gentle and—"

She went on in this manner for several minutes, while Reva smiled tenderly. Yet her heart was full of trouble. Once she, too, had been full of joy, confident that the world was hers. But the blissful dream had crumbled to dust. Then she gave herself a little shake.

Nicoletta was still talking. "Everybody will be there, and I will be so nervous..."

"I'm sorry." Reva gave herself a little shake. "Everybody will be where?"

"At the reception we're giving for the Torvinis. Oh, Reva, it matters so much that everything should be perfect that night. And then the count will give his consent, and Guido and I can be married soon."

Reva frowned. "Don't you mind having to do all this to convince the Torvinis that you're good enough for their son? Is *he* good enough for you?"

"I'm in love, *mia sorella*," Nicoletta said with simple dignity, "and love has no pride. Besides, I'm a Corelli, and the Corellis never give up what they have set their hearts on. My mother used to say that often."

"I thought you never knew your mother?"

Nicoletta nodded. "She died soon after I was born. But Demetrio talked about her a lot, because he said he wanted me to know our mother, even though she was dead. He told me many times that she taught him never to admit defeat. He says this is why he is successful now."

"Hmm... I think his own nature might have had something to do with it," Reva said wryly.

Nicoletta laughed. "Oh, yes. But my aunt, who looked after me, says Mamma was just the same, full of vision and very determined. She said some people thought Mamma was hard, but not those who knew her and loved her. I think Demetrio is like her in that, too."

Something significant in her voice made Reva say quickly, "I'm just here to play my part."

"Oh, I know. You've come because you're my dear, kind sister. But when Demetrio told me how quickly you agreed to help me, I think—" she looked slyly into Reva's face "—I think perhaps you came for you, too?"

There was no possible answer to this. Demetrio had cleverly misinformed his sister, making it impossible for Reva to speak her mind. "Let's leave that subject," she said hastily.

"Of course," Nicoletta said impishly. "Demetrio must wait and suffer. He deserves it."

She reverted to the subject of Guido, who, despite his charm, began to take on an alarming shape in Reva's mind. He seemed to have little independent existence. Even his job came to him by his father's favor, for Guido worked in the firm that controlled the Torvini family interests—another reason why he had to be so cautious about offending the count. Reva wondered what would happen if he had to stand on his own feet, and if Nicoletta had ever worried about that.

At last she said, "It's time I unpacked."

"Shall I send my maid?"

"Thank you, but I'll do it myself."

"Then I shall help you."

"All right, but you'll be scandalized by my lack of high fashion. You always were."

She was right. Nicoletta was too polite to express her true opinion of Reva's functional wardrobe, but her looks spoke volumes.

Suddenly Reva gave a huge yawn. The lack of sleep she'd been fighting off seemed to have caught up with her.

"You were flying in the night," Nicoletta said sympathetically. "I'll send you some breakfast, and then you can sleep."

"Just tea, please," Reva said gratefully. "Tell Demetrio I'm sorry, but I won't be down for a while."

"Demetrio has gone," Nicoletta said. "He went straight back to his office. And he says he'll probably be late tonight, because he has to make up the time he lost this morning."

How like Demetrio, Reva thought wryly as Nicoletta sailed out. Having achieved one goal, he went straight on to the next. That was all she was, a goal to be achieved, and he'd achieved her with all his usual efficiency and lack of scruples. But then she thought of what Nicoletta had told her, and with her mind's eye she could see him, a very young man, talking earnestly to the little girl about their mother, trying to preserve the beloved memory. The two aspects didn't add up. Yet, somehow, they must.

Then she remembered that she was only going to be here for a short while, and nothing to do with Demetrio concerned her any longer.

She dozed for most of the day, then dressed for dinner and went down to chat to Nicoletta while they waited for Demetrio. As he'd predicted, he was late, and it was almost nine o'clock by the time they sat down. Reva tried to appear pleasant and at ease, but she was conscious of the servants' curious eyes upon her. She talked mostly with Nicoletta. Demetrio seemed preoccupied.

When the meal was over, Nicoletta looked surreptitiously at her watch, then at her brother, then at Reva. Demetrio gave an unexpected grin. "Go on," he said. "I'm sure Reva will excuse you—if he's still there by now."

"He'll be there," Nicoletta said eagerly. "Reva... I know it's your first evening and I should be polite, but..."

"Go on," Reva said, smiling.

The girl fled like a whirlwind, leaving the two of them facing each other across the large table. Demetrio looked tired, she realized, and the lights made hollows in his cheeks. "Thank you for being understanding," he said. "They spend most evenings together, but when they can't he always waits for her by the gate."

"Don't you ask him in?" Reva enquired.

"He doesn't want to come in. He wants to be alone with her." A silence fell between them. "You realize we're under observation?" he said at last.

"I've been realizing it all evening."

"We're expected to take our coffee together in the music room. A minimum of fifteen minutes is required."

"Then let's do what's expected," she said lightly.

In the music room, a servant was already laying out the coffee things on a low table. Demetrio dismissed him and served Reva himself. "I called Count Torvini today," he said. "I invited him and his family to a reception in their honor in this house in two weeks' time. He accepted, and said he was looking forward to renewing your acquaintance."

"I'll do my best not to let Nicoletta down," she said.

Demetrio felt in an inside pocket of his jacket, produced an envelope, and handed it to her. "What's this?" she asked.

"Our business agreement. I said I'd pay you for your services."

The envelope contained a bank book with a large amount credited to an account in her name. "I'd rather not," she said coolly. "I prefer to earn my money independently."

"Yes, you always preferred going your own way," he said with a flash of irony. "In fact, you preferred anything to acting like a wife."

"That's not true."

"It is from my point of view. But forget that. I didn't mean to attack you. I resolved not to, and I won't break that resolve again."

It was easier said than done, he reflected as he sipped his coffee. He'd made a thousand resolutions about how he should act, but the sight of her seemed to drive them from his mind. There she stood, looking at him defensively, her head held high on her long neck, her whole pose redolent of a kind of 'damn you' arrogance that he'd once found fascinating. Now all he saw was the barrier it formed.

To his annoyance, she placed the envelope on the mantelpiece and turned away. Her rejection rekindled his bitterness, reminding him how she'd killed his love. Anger rose in him. How he longed to pay her back in her own coin, to make her suffer as she had made him suffer. But he couldn't do it, because her cool English feelings had never been the equal of his. She could match him hatred for hatred and passion for passion, but she had never matched him love for love. She'd told him so, had gloried in telling him so.

He rose swiftly, seizing her wrist. "Let go of me at once," she said coldly.

The expression in her eyes devastated him. How could a woman look like that at a man, when she had once lain beneath him, holding him inside her, crying his name in pleading ecstasy? How could she give him all the little precious touches that incited his passion and then look at him now with eyes like stones?

Without releasing her, he took the envelope and pushed it into her hand. "Take it," he said harshly. "It's part of our bargain."

"I made no bargain about money."

He scarcely heard the words. He was aware of nothing but the movement of her lips, reminding him how they had moved that morning beneath his own, reluctantly but helplessly.

He'd approached their first meeting coolly and with everything laid out in his mind. She was an enemy to be conquered, a rival to negotiate with in order to secure a deal in his favor. He had made many such deals.

But his calculations had gone awry when he'd found her nearly naked. Her endlessly long legs, whose beauty had always excited him, had been in full view, driving everything else out of his head. He'd sworn not to touch her, to say what he had to say calmly and with composure. But her nearness had destroyed that resolve, and that moment when he'd held her close to him had shaken him to the core. She had responded, however she tried to deny it. She might not care for him, but her body still belonged to him. They both knew it, and she couldn't forgive him for it.

Then let her not forgive, he thought harshly. Let her hate him as much as she liked, as long as she returned to his bed. Briefly he recalled the promise he'd made her that morning, but he dismissed it. To hell with promises. He wanted her, and he would have her. "Stop pretending, Reva," he said, still holding her. "This isn't about money, or about bargains, it's about us. You know what happened this morning. You know there's still something there." It was there now, he thought exultantly, feeling her pulse race beneath his fingers.

But her voice was cold. "Not the right thing," she said. "Nothing that matters."

"Damn you, don't insult me! You've been in my bed. You know what matters."

"I know that some things matter less than they seem to at the time," she snapped, "and I'm never going to let myself be fooled again."

"Reva, listen to me, and listen well, for I'll never make this offer again. Agree to let bygones be bygones, and I'll take you back and treat you as well as if you'd never let me down. Do you understand? I'm willing to forgive and forget."

"But I'm not." Her voice cut him like a whip. "I'll never forgive or forget, Demetrio, and if you don't let go this instant I'll walk out of here tonight."

Slowly his fingers loosened and he released her. He was shaking. "I told you I'd never make such an offer again," he said. "You had your chance."

"And I've only myself to blame for not taking it, haven't I?" she said, with a hint of mockery that stabbed him. "This arrangement will only be tolerable if we keep each other at a distance."

"In that case, you should accept my money," he said, recovering some of his composure. "That makes it a business bargain."

She surveyed him ironically. "All right. On those terms." She moved away from him, the envelope in her hand. "And there's one other thing. There's a connecting door to our rooms."

"Don't worry. It's safely locked."

"I want all the keys to it."

"I won't open that door. You have my promise."

Reva smiled wryly. "I remember hearing you talk very eloquently on the subject of promises given under duress. According to you, they don't count. I want the keys, Demetrio—every single one of them."

Slightly to her surprise, he was prepared. Reaching into his pocket, he came out with two large keys, which he put into her hand. "That's all there are," he said. "And that's a promise that you can believe or not, as you like."

"All right. I'll believe it."

"There's one more thing." He left her and went to his study. A heavy black safe stood in the corner. He opened it and extracted a large, flat box, which he carried back to Reva.

She gasped when he opened it. Inside, on a background of black velvet, was a set of jewelry that defied imagination. Necklace, earrings, bracelet, tiara, all made of the most perfect diamonds. They glittered and dazzled, half blinding her with the intensity of their white fire.

"I want you to wear these at the reception," he said in a toneless voice. "I show them to you now so that you can bear these in mind when ordering your dress. You understand that my wife must outshine every other woman."

"I understand perfectly. Where on earth did you—? You didn't—?"

"No, I didn't buy them especially for you," he replied smoothly. "They belong to this estate. Tomorrow they'll be returned to the bank, to be taken out again the day before the reception. I also have these for you." He placed a set of car keys on the mantelpiece. "A car has been set aside for your use while you're here." He consulted his watch, like a man who'd given enough time to an item on his agenda. "Now, if you'll forgive me, I have to do some work."

"By all means," she said politely.

She remained, drinking coffee, for a few more minutes. Then Nicoletta returned, her hair in slight disarray and her eyes shining. She sang Guido's praises for half an hour. Reva was finding it an increasing strain. She wanted to join in Nicoletta's happiness, but it was as though she could see a pit yawning at the girl's feet, and nobody else knew it was there. So she made an excuse and went to bed, lest she should blurt out the wrong remark.

Demetrio remained in his study long after he heard Reva go up the stairs. The house was quiet as he went to his own room. As he got undressed, he happened to catch a glimpse of himself in a mirror. The angle revealed his back, which still showed the marks Reva had made on it with her fingernails that morning. The sight caused him to give a grimace of dissatisfaction with himself. If she'd revealed her need, so had he. The sensation of her clinging to him had felt good. It had felt better than anything else had in the past year, and it had evoked memories. In the past, some of their physical encounters had been sweet and tender, but others had resembled battles, leaving them both exhausted and yet eager for more. He missed those glorious battles. No other woman had ever inspired him to such vigor. For a moment, that morning, it had seemed as if everything were being given back to him, but the moment had been fleeting. She'd turned against him with bewildering suddenness.

He groaned as he remembered how, only an hour ago, he'd invited her back, offering to forgive and forget, and she'd snubbed him. How could he have so easily forgotten the first principle of negotiation? *Never* be the first one to blink. That rule had brought him victoriously through a thousand tough deals, and yet with this woman, the last person with whom he dared show weakness, he'd lowered his guard.

But only briefly. It wouldn't happen again. He'd lost a small battle—not the war.

* * *

Reva left the house immediately after breakfast the next morning, drove into Milan and straight to the building that housed *Domani*. There she headed for the editor's office. "My name is Reva Horden, and I'm here to see Signor Luciani," she told the secretary.

The secretary leafed through her appointment book with a puzzled frown. "Is he expecting you?" she asked at last.

"Seeing that he flew me from England for the express purpose of getting me to work for him, I think you could say he's expecting me," Reva said.

The secretary flicked a switch on the intercom and spoke to the editor. When she had explained Reva's presence, there was a sudden dead silence from the other end. Then Luciani, sounding disconcerted, said, "Ask Signora Corelli to come in."

Adolfo Luciani was a balding middle-aged man. He was waiting by the door, and he grasped Reva's hand in a simulation of welcome. But she wasn't fooled. He was uneasy at seeing her here. "Not Signora Corelli," she said. "Signorina Horden. That's the name under which you hired me. So, now I'm here to start work."

His uneasiness grew more marked. "Haven't you seen your husband since you arrived?"

"My husband has nothing to do with it. I'm a working photographer, and I'm here to work. You hired me. I have your letters to prove it, and I've gone to a lot of trouble to be available." Then, as the man appeared about to expire in misery, she relented. "Yes, I've seen my husband, and I know all about the trick you conspired to play on me."

"'Conspired' is an unhappy choice of word, *signora*—" Meeting her eyes, he hastily said, *"signorina."*

"It's a perfect choice of word," Reva said firmly. "Furthermore, it was thoroughly unethical for you to allow the magazine's name to be used in such a way. I wonder how your publisher would feel if he knew."

"Very unhappy," Luciani admitted, mopping his brow.

"Well, he need never know, as long as you stick to the terms of our agreement and give me some work."

"I dare not," he said unhappily. "I promised your husband."

At that Reva lost her temper. She lost it in Italian, which she now spoke fluently, and for two minutes she delivered a stream of colorful Italian invective that made Luciani look at her with new respect. But he wouldn't budge. Clearly his dread of Demetrio's wrath outweighed all other considerations.

"Are you really so afraid of Demetrio Corelli?" she asked at last.

"Everyone is afraid of Demetrio Corelli, *signorina.* Except perhaps you."

"More afraid of him than of your boss? He's not the publisher, is he? Or is he? Don't tell me he's bought *Domani* as well?"

"Oh, no," Luciani said quickly. "But you see . . ." He hesitated, clearly very unhappy.

"It will be much better for you to tell me than for me to investigate and find out," Reva pointed out.

Luciani groaned. "Between the two of you, it is like being squeezed by pincers," he complained. "May I say, in passing, that you are well matched?"

"You may say nothing of the sort. It isn't true. Now, what sort of hold does he have over you?"

"I have my little weaknesses, *signorina*. I gamble—perhaps more than I should."

"You mean you've lost a fortune?" Reva asked shrewdly.

He nodded. "My wife...she knows nothing...and she must not."

"Are you telling me," Reva demanded, "that Demetrio Corelli is threatening to tell your wife?"

"It's worse than that, *signorina*. He has bought up all my debts. If I 'act like a friend' to him, he will write them off and I shall be free."

"But if you step out of line he'll go and worry your poor little wife?" Reva asked, aghast.

This description of his other half seemed to revive Luciani. "My 'poor little wife' is nearly six feet tall and is twin sister to a heavyweight wrestler," he said desperately.

Despite her annoyance, Reva's lips twitched. Luciani was five foot six, and weedily built. "I see the problem," she said. "All right. There's no need to tell me any more." She got up to go.

"You won't give me away, will you, *signorina?*" he begged. "My life is difficult enough as it is."

She sighed. "No, I won't tell anyone. It's not your fault."

She left quickly, feeling frustrated and furious. She had always known that Demetrio was a powerful man, a man other men feared, but it was only now that that power was being exercised on herself that she understood how pervasive it was.

Her anger was so intense that for a moment she almost thought he was there with her. The air seemed to crackle with the electric excitement of his presence. Last night they'd fought a battle of wills, and the outcome had been about even. But she'd left him resolved to get work and use as little of his money as possible, and he knew her well enough to guess that. Now he seemed to be beside her, challenging her with his power, the power that had bent and broken so many enemies.

"But not me," she vowed. "You never had an enemy like me, Demetrio. You managed to get me here, but I'll fight you every moment—and I'll win."

Four

As she reached the outer door, she heard a voice calling her and turned to look back. A thin, untidy man was pursuing her. "Hello," he said in English when he caught up. "My name is Benno Andrese."

Reva took the hand he held out to her. "I'm Reva Horden," she said.

"I know. I'm a free-lance journalist. I read many foreign publications, and I'm a great admirer of your work. I've often wished I could work with you, but I suppose *Domani* has the exclusive use of your services."

"Not at all," Reva said, feeling a rising excitement. "I think we could work very well together."

"Let's have a drink and talk about it."

"All right. That would be nice."

They found a small bar and Benno ordered aperitifs for them. While he was paying for them, she studied him. He seemed to be in his late forties, and he had a look she was used to in journalists, that of having lived a hectic life and having gotten a bit battered in the process.

"I knock about, earning a crust wherever I can," he told her when he returned. "Mostly I spend it as soon as I earn it. That's why I was haunting the offices of *Domani* this morning. They pay better than anyone else. The trouble is, they play safe. *Domani* means *tomorrow,* but it's been a while since that magazine has been forward-looking. Adolfo's a good fellow, but he's scared of his own shadow."

"I know. I came here expecting to work for him, but the offer has suddenly been withdrawn," Reva said, choosing her words carefully.

"He won't buy much of my stuff. It isn't bland enough for him. I like to hunt around in corners and turn over stones to see what's scuttling about underneath. The best news story is one that someone, somewhere, is furious about."

"That's just how I feel," she said at once. "My— Somebody recently said of me that if there was no one trying to snatch my camera away or club me over the head I got bored."

They grinned at each other in perfect mutual understanding. "But you're not just a photographer," he pointed out. "That Michael Denton story had me green with envy. So full of precise detail. It was the best thing you ever did."

"I disagree," Reva said, a mite coolly.

"Come on. Admit it. It made your name. I thought you'd follow up with some more exposés, but you never did."

Reva sipped her drink to hide her chagrin. It was annoying to be told that Demetrio's input had done so much for her career. "That story was a one-off," she said at last. "I had access to certain information, but after that my informant—" she hesitated "—wasn't available."

"Are you sure there wasn't another reason?" Benno asked quizzically.

"Whatever do you mean?"

"Well..." Benno seemed to be treading cautiously. "You rather...went over to the other side, didn't you?"

"Other side?"

"The side of the wealthy and privileged, where Demetrio Corelli lives."

Reva opened her mouth to say it was all a charade, but stopped. The Milanese grapevine was too efficient for her to take risks.

Benno went on. "I can understand that, whatever Reva Horden might want to do, exposé journalism could be difficult for Signora Corelli."

Reva drew a deep, furious breath. Was she always going to be dogged by that hated name? "Have you ever seen the name Corelli on my work?" she asked.

"No, but facts are facts. You *are* Signora Corelli, and everyone knows it."

"Let's get one thing clear," she said firmly. "When I'm working, I'm *not* Signora Corelli. In fact, I'm not even going to be Reva Horden, since that name, too, seems to be compromised by association. I'll choose another, one that nobody knows."

"Such as what?"

She thought for a moment. "My mother wanted me to be a dancer, so after Reva she named me after all her favorite ballerinas—Margot, Alicia, Antoinette..."

"Alicia's nice."

"Fine. I'll be Alicia."

"Alicia who?"

"Just Alicia. Let's keep it mysterious."

"But how will you get paid?"

"Through you. You can be my agent when we work together, and the publisher will pay you."

"It won't be much," he warned. "I mostly work for *Time & Tide*. It's a great little magazine—specializes in exposing corrupt politicians. The trouble is, it's produced on a shoestring and pays peanuts. But it tells the truth. Look, how would you like to do something so difficult, and perhaps dangerous, that three other photographers have already turned it down?"

"Sounds right up my street," she said at once.

Benno named a well-known soft drink factory. "You wouldn't believe some of the things that go on there," he said. "I know for a fact that they're using a process that's forbidden by law. It's just a matter of showing them up."

"How do you know about all this?"

"I have a 'mole.' He'll let us in."

"What are we waiting for?"

"Just a moment. I'll call him."

He went to the phone at the bar and talked for a minute. When he returned, he said, "Let's go."

In half an hour they were slipping in through a side entrance of the factory, opened for them by the nervous "mole." He hurried them into white coats and hats, all the while looking over his shoulder. When they were dressed, they slipped in among the workers, who were all attired the same way. Reva glided here and there, snatching shots where Benno indicated, until their guide showed them through a door, which he promptly shut behind them. "You've got five minutes," he said, clearly agitated.

A horrible smell was coming from the process under way, but Reva swallowed her sickness and snapped away madly while Benno muttered notes into a small recorder. Suddenly the air was split by the noise of a klaxon. "Shift break," muttered the guide. "Someone will arrive any moment. Get the hell out of here."

In a few minutes they were outside, breathing in lungfuls of fresh air.

"Hey, you!" came a voice from above their heads. "What are you doing on this property? Security!"

"Time for us to go," Benno muttered, seizing her hand.

"They're closing the gate," Reva cried.

"Can you climb?"

"Watch me."

"There's the wall. Here we go."

A door opened, and four dogs came tearing out, fangs showing, eyes blazing. They both took a flying leap at the high wall that barred their exit. Reva nearly dropped back, but clung on frantically with one hand while Benno hauled her up and the dogs snapped at her ankles. As she dropped down the other side, she could hear the animals howling in frustration. They ran until they were breathless, and when it seemed safe to stop they looked behind them. There were no pursuers. Reva leaned against a wall, gasping. Her blood sang with excitement. This was how she liked it.

"I've got to go home and start writing," Benno said. "I'll meet you in that bar tomorrow morning, and you can give me the pictures. I hope they're good."

"They will be," Reva promised.

She said goodbye to him and made her way back to where her car was parked. On the way home she stopped off at a photographic equipment shop and made some purchases. She bought one more item at a locksmith's shop, before heading back to the Palazzo Corsevo. When she turned in at the gate, she was humming to herself.

She'd been so preoccupied that she hadn't noticed time passing, and now it was early afternoon—siesta time. The house lay quiet in the baking heat, and she had privacy to look over the place. To her delight, she managed to hunt down and take over an extra kitchen that nobody used, but where the running water was still functioning. It took two hours of hard work to black out all the windows, fix a new lock on the door and arrange everything as she wanted it, but when she'd finished she had an adequate darkroom.

She turned the key in the lock and set to work. Time and place vanished as she developed her film and made enlargements of the best pictures. At last she stood back and regarded them with satisfaction.

Only then did she become aware of a commotion outside. She opened the door and listened. The whole house seemed to be in an uproar. She saw a maid scurrying past and stopped her. "What's hap—?" she began.

She got no further. At the sight of her face the maid gave a violent start and ran away shrieking, "The *signora* is here. The *signora* is here."

Reva stared after her. Then she realized that she could see darkness through a window that looked out onto the grounds. It had been broad daylight when she shut herself away in her darkened room. Now it was late evening.

Demetrio appeared, very pale. "Where the devil have you been?" he demanded. "Everyone has been looking for you for the last two hours."

"Oh, dear," Reva said guiltily. "I've been developing film. I'm afraid I got absorbed and forgot the time."

"You—" Demetrio seemed to have trouble finding his voice. "Do you realize," he said at last, "that I—that we have all been worried for you? I had the cellars searched in case you'd got lost in there or had a fall. Have you *no* consideration?"

"I'm sorry," she said helplessly. "I really am."

Demetrio's eyes glinted unpleasantly. "*Sorry* is an easy word to say, Reva. You always relied on it when you wanted me to understand why I came at the bottom of your list of priorities."

He turned away. Reva hurried and caught up with him as he reached the front door. "It was unforgivably rude of me," she agreed. "I'll be more careful another time."

"Why are you developing film, anyway?" he demanded.

"Because, despite your efforts to stop me, I've found some work to do."

He halted at the door to his bedroom. "What work?"

"Oh, no. I'm not telling you any more. I don't want to find this avenue blocked off, as well."

"I see no reason for you to work."

"I see every reason," Reva retorted quickly.

"Then let me make it plain that while you're here I don't expect you to—" He halted, because Reva's ironic eyes on him were like a warning. "Do what you damned well please," he snapped, and started to go down the steps.

"Where are you going?" she cried.

"I'm going back to my office. I may as well be there as here."

Reva watched in dismay as he got into the car and swung it away down the drive. She turned back and found Nicoletta waiting for her just inside the house.

"I'm sorry," she said again. "I should have realized nobody knew where I was, but I just got carried away."

Nicoletta nodded, smiling. "I remember how you used to vanish inside yourself to a place where no one could reach you. You're an artist, and you can't be other than you are. My stupid brother should have realized that. Don't take any notice if he makes a fuss."

Reva found herself perversely arguing the other way. "I suppose he's got a right to make a fuss." Then a horrible thought struck her. "We didn't have guests tonight, did we?"

"No, it's all right. But perhaps you should be nice to Antonio. He cooked your favorite soufflé and now it's ruined."

Reva promptly visited the kitchen and apologized to Antonio. He gave her to understand that his feelings were wounded, but allowed himself to be placated, and launched into a flood of detail about his efforts to get the soufflé just as the *signora* liked it.

"How did you know how I liked it?" Reva asked curiously.

"Signor Corelli told me—" Antonio suddenly checked himself, floundering. "He told me...told me to study the notes left by my predecessor. I found in them full details of your likes and dislikes."

"I see. Thank you, Antonio." Reva was too taken aback to say more.

She went to her room at eleven o'clock that night, but at first she didn't undress. Demetrio was bound to return soon, and she wanted to apologize to him for her thoughtlessness. It was clear that he'd told Antonio to prepare her favorite dish, and that made her feel even worse about what had happened tonight. But then she realized she was being foolishly sentimental, and sentimentality was the one thing most likely to arouse Demetrio's derision. There was nothing personal in his actions. He was always well organized and efficient, and it was in his own interests to keep her content here.

She undressed and got into bed. But it was an hour before she could stop herself straining to hear the sound of his car returning. At long last she fell asleep.

Demetrio cursed when he heard the sound of a police siren and saw the light in his rearview mirror. He'd driven too fast as he left the villa, and he'd stepped on the gas as he headed down the road into Milan. He knew it was useless. It would take more than a fast car to escape the Furies that pursued him.

Reva's apparent disappearance had plunged him into a black hell that was terrifyingly like that other time he'd come home and found her gone. He'd been possessed by the conviction that she'd changed her mind and gone back to England. It had been no comfort that her car was there. She could have slipped away on foot. He'd made a frantic search of his own room, then hers, seeking a note that would tell him she'd left him again. It had been little comfort not to find one. His mind had promptly discovered new terrors.

The anticlimax of finding that she had been there all the time, the discovery that she had blotted him out of her consciousness so easily, and the knowledge that he had revealed his anxiety, all combined to fill him with a violent emotion that he hadn't dared let her see. He'd fled her, seeking the solace of work, the one thing that had never failed him. But he'd run straight into trouble with the law.

He pulled over and found his driver's license as the policeman approached him. "Do you know what speed you were— Oh, *Dio mio!* Signor Corelli!"

Demetrio looked up at the fresh-faced boy and recognized Claudio, the son of one of his best workers. "Yes, I know what I was doing," he said. "And it was way over the limit."

"I'm sure it wasn't, *signore,*" the boy said hastily.

"You thought it was when you stopped me."

"I must have been mistaken."

"You weren't mistaken," Demetrio said in mild exasperation. "You were going to give me a ticket, so give me a ticket. I don't ask for privileged treatment any more than I give it."

"Forgive me *signore,* but my papa told me that when he had that heart attack it was you who paid all—"

"Get on with it." Demetrio cut him short firmly.

"Yes, *signore.*" The young policeman handed him the ticket and returned to his motorcycle. As Demetrio's taillights vanished into the distance, he sat there and mopped his brow.

Demetrio let himself into the darkened office building, taking the lift that swept directly from the parking garage up to his office. He didn't put on the lights, but stood looking out the huge windows at the city. It was only a few days before that he'd stood in this very spot, savoring the triumph of knowing that his net was slowly closing over Reva, that every step she took was returning her to his power.

Now those calculations seemed futile and deluded. She was no more in his power than she had ever been. She'd demonstrated that today by shutting herself away and forgetting him. Once he'd thought to keep her by locking a door on her, but she could trump him by locking the door herself and keeping him out.

He thrust her out of his mind. New York was six hours behind Milan, so he could still do business. But after a couple of phone calls he stopped in the act of dialing the third number and put the receiver down. His mind wasn't on what he was doing. It was fixed on the little apartment next door, on the bed where he'd once known so much happiness, a bed that was now as cold and empty as his heart.

He found himself remembering a day, early in their marriage, when he'd had to go to New York. He'd wanted her to go with him, but she'd insisted on sticking to a photographic assignment that she'd previously agreed to. He'd been outraged, and on their last morning, what should have been a passionate farewell had turned into a quarrel. He'd stormed out and gone to the office for a day's work before leaving for the airport in the evening. Halfway through the afternoon, Reva had called him from a booth in the reception area downstairs.

"I'm coming up. Is your secretary with you?" she'd asked.

"Yes."

"Make sure she's not there when I arrive."

The husky, throbbing quality in her voice had told him everything, but he'd still been startled when she appeared, locked the door behind her and began to strip.

"Reva," he'd exclaimed, half laughing, half delighted, "what will my staff be think—?" The last word had been cut off by her mouth on his, and the next moment he, too, had been tearing off his clothes. At first they couldn't even make it as far as the bedroom, but had enjoyed each other on the thick rug. They'd been voracious, making love with hungry intensity. When it was over, she'd sighed and said, "I guess that's going to have to last me."

"Come to New York with me," he'd pleaded.

She'd sighed again. "If only I could."

"Come with me," he'd repeated insistently.

But she hadn't budged, although her yearning to be with him had been genuine. She'd proved that again before she'd left, this time in the bed. As often before she'd had him thoroughly confused. She'd been his wife, but she'd acted like a mistress, seducing him on the floor of his own office in the middle of the afternoon, then going her own independent way. Through the haze of sexual delight, he'd failed to heed the warning signals. He'd been so sure that in time she would settle down and become like the wives of his business colleagues, who never put anything before their duty to their husbands and their husbands' firms. Now he wondered how he could have been so naive.

It was past midnight. What would she be doing? Suddenly he fiercely regretted leaving her. He might return to find she'd really left. His blood ran cold, and he reached for the phone. He would call Nicoletta to say good-night, and she would alert him if anything was wrong.

But he stayed his hand. However he disguised the call, Reva would know and understand the implications. It would be another victory to her, and after last night he didn't dare concede a second point to that beautiful, maddening, enchanting and thoroughly impossible woman.

Abruptly he got up. In moments he'd descended the lift and was heading out of the parking garage toward the villa.

It was nearly one when he arrived, and the villa was in darkness. He let himself in through a side door and walked quietly up the stairs. He paused outside Reva's bedroom door and stood listening, trying to discern the sound of her breathing. He could hear nothing, and at last he tentatively tried the handle. The door was firmly locked.

Once in his own room, he stripped and showered, trying to wash the day away. When he'd toweled himself dry, he donned a light silk robe and threw himself onto the bed. It was late, and he was worn out, but he knew he couldn't sleep. The day's events had left his nerves stretched almost to the breaking point.

He couldn't prevent himself turning his eyes to the connecting door. Her bed was nearer to this door than to the other. He would be able to hear her breathing.

But there was no sound even when he pressed his ear against the crack. This door, too, was locked. He tried to still his rising fear. Of course she was there. She must be inside, to have locked the door.

No, whispered the demon in his mind, *she's clever enough to have locked it from the outside when she went away, just to fool you.*

He must keep his sense of proportion, which was one of his most vital weapons in any situation. It had given him an instinct for what mattered and what didn't, and he'd won many a battle by shrewdly sacrificing a pawn.

But his sense of proportion had deserted him, to be replaced by dread. Only one thing mattered. Was Reva on the other side of that door, or had she deserted him again? He *had* to know the answer to that, whatever he needed to do to find out.

Turning out the light, he went to the floor-length windows that opened out on his stone balcony. In the moonlight he could see Reva's balcony, and her own windows. To his relief, one of them stood slightly open.

The balconies didn't connect, but there were only two feet between them. Moving as silently as a panther, he climbed up onto the rail and took a long stride across the gap. Gently, hardly breathing, he pushed open the tall window.

The room was dark except for a shaft of moonlight that streamed across one side of the bed. There was no one there, but the other side was still in darkness. From this angle it was impossible to see if the bedclothes had been disturbed. He moved softly toward the bed.

Now he could hear her breathing, and the relief was so great that he clutched a nearby dresser. He would risk just one more step in order to see her.

At that moment she gave a little gasp and turned over in the bed, pushing the bedclothes away from her. The movement brought her into the patch of moonlight. Demetrio grew very still when he saw that she was wearing nothing. She had often slept like this in the hot Italian night, covered only by a sheet that she often flung off eventually. Now the sheet covered her to just below the waist. Above that, she was naked, stretched out on her back, her head moving restlessly in the heat.

His heart was thumping painfully as he saw her lying as she had so often lain beneath him. The dark areolae of her nipples were clear against her pale skin, which gleamed with a pearly sheen in the moonlight.

Demetrio stood watching her, in a state of near shock. In the time since Reva's return he'd seen caution, mistrust and rejection in her face. But at this moment her attitude of defenseless abandon brought back memories of a thousand lovings in hot, velvet nights, of sweet words whispered in his ear, of eager, passionate pleading, "Now, Demetrio...*now*...*now*... Oh, my love...my love..."

There was an unaccustomed ache in his throat. He wanted to stay here forever, drinking in her beauty, pretending she was still his, but he didn't dare. Suddenly she turned restlessly in her sleep, flinging out an arm. Her hand brushed against him and stopped, resting against his sleeve.

He froze. If she should awaken and see him here, it would be a disaster. Cautiously he brought forward his other hand and took hold of hers, meaning to lay it gently back on the bed. But she gripped him strongly and pulled him forward until he was forced to move closer and sit on the edge of the bed. She still didn't wake, but kept hold of him, drawing his hand to her breast.

Demetrio's heart almost stopped. This was one of her old signals. In the days when their passion had flowed as freely as summer wine, she'd often taken his hand to lay it on her breast in a wordless message of desire. That time had seemed so far away in the past couple of days, when she'd been cold and hostile to him. But now, when she was asleep and her guard was down, she was her true self again. And her true self wanted him.

He should have dressed before coming here, he realized. Hot tremors were chasing each other over the surface of his skin, and the awareness of being almost naked, in the presence of her nakedness, was almost too much for his control. In the past, that very control had been a potent sexual weapon. He'd used it to prolong the moments of ecstasy in a way she loved, making her wait for the climax, which was twice as explosive when it came. Now he needed all his strength to keep from throwing off his robe and drawing her body against his, claiming her heated flesh in a way that had always made things right before. It would be so simple....

The sensation of the soft fullness in his palm again, after so long, was unbearably good. He could feel the nipple grow hard and peaked with desire, and he knew from memory everything else that was happening to her now. He knew that if he laid his head against her breast he would hear the deep, soft thundering of her heart. How often in the past had he heard that sound, and rejoiced, knowing that her beautiful body was waiting for him with joy! And then it had been so natural to slip between her parted legs and enter her, feeling the heat of her loins envelop him with fierce, surging passion. That heat would be there now, he was certain. He had only to draw back the sheet and run gentle fingers up the silky surface of her inner thigh until they reached the place that he still thought of as his home—the place that would always be his home.

Tremors went through him as he thought of what might happen in a few seconds. He reached out his free hand, but then Reva did something that stopped him in his tracks. She sighed.

It was a gentle sigh, almost inaudible, but he heard it, and he drew in a sharp breath. His pulse was racing. He wanted her, with a deep, hungry craving. The bitter resentment at what she'd done to him was as strong as ever, but it warred with a raw need that invaded his loins and turned him to fire. The thought of the lovely body half-hidden by the thin sheet, so near and yet so far, made something catch in his throat so that he could hardly breathe. She was his wife. She belonged to him, didn't she?

But she had sighed, and the soft sound had a wistful, defenseless quality that clutched at his heart. Suddenly it was impossible for him to go on. Gently he began to withdraw his hand from her breast, but she seemed to protest, folding her own hands over his and throwing back her head in a remembered gesture of pleading and seduction. It was almost his undoing, but he still fought for control.

Gently he leaned down and whispered, "It's all right... you're only dreaming... only dreaming..."

Whether it was the words, or the sound of his voice, he didn't know, but she grew calm, and the restlessness seemed to leave her. With a superhuman effort, he drew away from her and quietly left the room.

The sunlight on her face awoke Reva, and as soon as she opened her eyes she was filled with a marvelous sense of well-being. It flooded over her, suffusing every inch of her body with pleasure. She tried to recall when she'd last felt so good, and discovered, to her surprise, that her mind had to reach a long way back. The past year had contained its satisfactions and triumphs, but nothing like this singing awareness of joy.

She didn't know why she should feel like this, but she couldn't stop herself smiling. On impulse she took up her little bedside mirror and watched her features being taken over by a smile of impish delight. "Now why," she mused, "do I look like the cat that swallowed the cream?"

The phrase touched a chord in her memory. When... where... who? Then it came to her.

"You look like the cat that swallowed the cream," Demetrio had said tenderly after their first lovemaking.

She had nibbled his ear, muttering, "More cream... more cream..." And he had obliged.

That was how it had always been. A night in Demetrio's arms could leave her with a sense of glorious fulfilment that left her relaxed and alert at the same time. But why should she remember that now?

She recalled the black thunder on his face when he'd stormed out last night, and the hard edge of anger in his voice. But there was another memory that teased the edge of her consciousness. In it he'd spoken to her gently and with a tenderness she hadn't heard for a long time, and a balm had fallen over her heart. She frowned, trying to place it. She hadn't seen him since he'd left the house yesterday evening. And yet...

She dressed quickly and hurried downstairs. It was suddenly important to see Demetrio, and discover what there might be in his eyes. She was possessed by the strangest feeling, as though something new and thrilling were starting in her life. She felt, not like the disillusioned wife she was, but like a young girl anxious to know if her chosen lover returned her feelings. It was absurd, but she didn't care about that. She *had* to see Demetrio.

She ran into the breakfast room, where the sun was streaming through tall windows. It seemed to shine straight into her heart, illuminating sad corners and banishing doubt. With every moment the feeling grew until she was possessed by an inexplicable happiness.

With the sun in her eyes, she couldn't make out details of the room. She knew only that she was going from darkness into light. "Demetrio," she cried gladly. "Demetrio, I—"

She stopped. Demetrio wasn't there. Only Nicoletta sat at the table. "He had to leave early," she said. "But see, he has left you a note."

Reva seized the envelope by her place and tore it open, reading eagerly. But then her joy faded, leaving behind a gaping black chasm. In a neat, formal hand, Demetrio had written, Pressure of work obliges me to be at the office around the clock for a while, so I shall sleep here next week, and return just before the reception. Should you need anything, please speak to my secretary. Demetrio.

Five

##

Reva had always loved Milan. Other people might wax lyrical about the beauty of Rome, but something in her energetic nature had responded instantly to this bustling northern city, which was the center of everything modern and exciting in Italy. Here were the head offices of industry, big business, publishing, art and fashion.

The coming reception was a major event in the city's glittering social life. The guest list included almost everyone of local importance, plus some government dignitaries who would be flying from Rome for the occasion. Once the invitations had gone out, every couture house in both Rome and Milan had been on standby.

Fashion looked good on Reva's tall, elegant figure, but in the past she'd resisted Nicoletta's entreaties to her to have clothes specially designed for her. Her restless nature made lengthy fittings an ordeal, and she preferred the couture houses' ready-to-wear shops. But this was special, and for once she had agreed to an exclusive creation.

"Where are we going?" she asked Nicoletta as they drove out together one morning.

"Wait and see," Nicoletta said teasingly. "I've found a new genius."

Soon they were in Milan, threading their way through the little cobbled streets between the Via della Spiga and the Via Monte Napoleone that made up the fashion district. At last they stopped in front of a small eighteenth-century building bearing the legend Primo.

"Primo says I'm too short for high fashion," Nicoletta said with a giggle, "but he will love you."

She was right. Primo was a willowy young man who cast eager professional eyes over Reva. "Do you know what jewels you will be wearing?" he asked.

"Yes. Diamonds."

"Bene." He studied her for a few minutes, then made some rapid sketches that he then presented to her. Reva's eyes opened at a drawing of a pencil-slim gown that seemed to vibrate on the page. "In black," Primo announced dramatically.

"You think black is my color?" Reva queried in surprise.

"Of course. The *signora* is not a young girl, but a woman of sophistication."

"I've always thought of myself as a bit of a hobo," Reva confessed.

"No, no," Primo told her imperiously. "A woman of experience." He studied her again, walking around her like a man considering a racehorse. "You have good shoulders," he declared at last. "We will show them off."

"Will we?" she asked faintly.

"The shoulders must be completely bare, except for the diamonds."

"It gets drafty in that big house in the evening," Reva said with a touch of defiance.

"Then you will have a small embroidered jacket to wear until the heat generated by five hundred people makes you wish to take it off," Primo explained patiently. All at once his face crumpled like a child's. "*Dio mio.* Five hundred people, all crushed together. What it does to the clothes is a crime."

In another instant the tearful child vanished, to be replaced by the steely professional. He moved Reva this way and that, giving orders like a sergeant major. He made her walk while he stood back to judge the effect. He produced bolts of material that he draped against her and studied with narrowed eyes. When she begged for some coffee, he vetoed the idea and produced champagne. "Now," he said finally, "when you return next week, I shall have a toile ready to be fitted onto you, and you will have lost five pounds."

"I thought I was slim already," Reva said rebelliously.

"True. But you are slim like an athlete. To wear one of *my* creations, you must be slim like a model. You will diet on grapefruit and champagne."

Reva glared at Nicoletta, who was choking with laughter, but in the next few days she found herself following Primo's advice. It wasn't hard, because she'd lost her appetite. She couldn't have explained why a sudden feeling of oppression seemed to have come over her. She hadn't seen Demetrio since the day she'd found his note at breakfast, and although his absence was a relief, she was aware of something vital missing, a sensation of incompleteness that left her strangely restless. She had no difficulty in losing weight.

On the day of her fitting, she arrived ten minutes early and sat down to wait, idly picking up a magazine that she found lying on a chair. "That's this week's issue of *Time & Tide*," the receptionist said. "The client just before you is married to a man who owns a food factory, and there's a piece about it in there. She's furious. She says it's all lies—which means most of it's probably true."

Reva skimmed through the pages and found her own photographs. She'd delivered them to Benno a week ago, and hadn't expected them to appear so soon. Now she saw that they'd come out well, exposing everything that the guilty manufacturer would have wanted kept secret. She knew a surge of pure professional pride.

In another moment, the client emerged. Her eyes glittered when she saw the magazine in Reva's hand. "Those terrible slanders," she moaned. "My husband is a man of position, but they dare attack him with these lies. Nobody is safe."

She continued in this vein for another five minutes, while Primo gently ushered her out without appearing to do so. He came back smiling wickedly. "She can call them lies if she likes," he said, "but those pictures leave no doubt."

"They're very clear," Reva said, in a voice that gave nothing away.

"Clear? They're devastating. Let's see who took them. Alicia. I've never heard of her."

"Do you have my toile?" she asked to get him off the subject.

In a moment he produced the toile, a dress made from coarse muslin and tacked together. He pinned it on her, then spent an hour making adjustments and barking instructions at an assistant, who took copious notes. Only when he was completely satisfied did he remove it and hand it over. It would now form the template from which the actual dress would be made.

"The fabric will be silk crêpe," he declared, showing her the material he'd selected. She handled it lovingly, wondering if she would look as wonderful in it as he promised, but then reflecting that it didn't really matter. It was Nicoletta who must look wonderful.

But try as she might to be blasé, she couldn't help feeling excited as the days passed and the beautiful garment was created for her. At the very next fitting, when the black crêpe was only tacked into shape, she could already glimpse the stunning creation that was evolving. After that, she was impatient for every fitting.

Four days before the reception, she reached home at lunchtime to find Francesca waiting for her on the steps, looking agitated. "*Signora,* there's a man asking to speak to you on the telephone." Her eyes were full of disapproval. Reva went to her room to take the call. It was Benno.

"Come out and meet me," he said. "I've got something to show you."

"What is it?"

"Just bring your cameras and lots of film. And wear your oldest working clothes." He gave her directions to the meeting place and hung up. In a few minutes Reva was on the road again.

Benno was waiting for her, standing by his car. When he saw her, he waved and got back inside. She followed him for the better part of an hour, while the streets grew shabbier. At last they stopped outside an apartment block and got out. "It's called Paradise House," Benno said. "It's an ironic name, as you'll discover. Keep your cameras hidden for a while. It doesn't do to look too well off here. Mind you, we should be all right. My contact will vouch for us."

As he spoke, a young man came out and approached them. He wore jeans and a vest, both very old, and his sandals looked as if they were falling apart. He introduced himself as Rico. "Come in," he said.

As soon as she was inside, Reva was gagging at the smell. "Drains," Benno told her. "The landlord never does anything about them."

"And the drains are the least of it," Rico added. "There are also rats, and in winter the rain gets in. Come and see."

It was a nightmare journey. In apartment after apartment they found walls thick with fungus or with gaping holes. "Will the people who live here mind if I take pictures?" Reva asked.

"They'll be glad of it," Rico said. "They are hoping you'll help them."

Reva had the sensation of moving through a nightmare. When she'd finished photographing the conditions, mothers would thrust their children at her to show rat bites. Once she actually found herself eyeball-to-eyeball with a defiant-looking rat. She aimed the lens directly at it, returning defiance for defiance. "Can't they force the landlord to do something about it?" she demanded.

"Perhaps, if they knew who the landlord was," Benno said. "They pay their rent to a man from an agency. Nobody knows who actually owns the block. And when we do know, it'll probably turn out to be a company, owned by another company. Tracing ownership back to the source won't be easy, but I'm damned well going to try."

When they left, Rico said, "So now you have your story and your dramatic pictures, and you will publish them. And then, perhaps, you will forget us."

"No," Benno said at once. "I'm going to keep on until I find out who's behind this. That's a promise."

On the way home, they stopped for a coffee, and Benno said to Reva, "Are you sure you want to travel all the way on this one?"

"Of course. Why wouldn't I?"

He shrugged. "It just occurred to me that perhaps I wasn't very fair to involve Demetrio Corelli's wife."

After a moment, his meaning got home to her, and she shook her head firmly. "Not a chance. My husband would never be responsible for a scandal like that."

"Are you sure he's not the ultimate owner? He has a lot of property. Do you know every single thing he owns? Come to think of it, does *he* know every single thing he owns? His interests are so diverse that he probably doesn't."

"You do him an injustice," Reva said with mild irony. "I can't imagine Demetrio not knowing every detail of his own interests. He's the most efficient man on earth." After a moment, something impelled her to add, "He's also decent and conscientious. He wouldn't tolerate conditions like we've seen today."

Benno grinned. "Are you going to tell me what a nice man he is? A lot of people would be surprised to hear that."

Something in his skeptical tone fired her indignation. "That's because 'a lot of people' don't know the first thing about him. He may not be a soft touch in a business deal, but the others aren't soft touches, either. He has honesty and integrity, and that's more than most of them can say."

Benno grinned. "Don't eat me alive. I'm sorry if I offended you. Of course, you know him better than anyone else."

"Yes," Reva said slowly. "Yes, of course."

She was thoughtful as she drove home. Benno's casual words had forced her to face how very little she knew Demetrio. In their year together, their passion had overwhelmed them. It was incredible how few actual conversations they'd had. Her assertion that he had honesty and integrity had been based more on instinct than on knowledge. Yet the instinct was very strong.

It was late when she got home. Demetrio's car was standing in the drive for the first time in over a week. The sight made her realize that dinner would be well advanced, and she wondered how he would greet her. Would he be irritated at her absence, or even, perhaps, glad to see her?

In fact, he was neither. She was met by Francesca, who told her that Demetrio had eaten in his study, leaving instructions that he wasn't to be disturbed.

So that was that, she thought. It was a relief to know that there would be no anger, no reproaches, no accusations of wifely indifference. But apparently there was also no interest, and she felt again the mysterious sense of oppression that had plagued her recently.

In the last few days before the reception, she had no time to dwell on her thoughts. She'd played little part in the preparations. Francesca was experienced in such occasions and Nicoletta knew the house better. But she was still *la padrona*, and there were a dozen minor decisions that apparently couldn't be settled until she had spoken. As the time grew near, she found herself becoming nervous. It was so important not to let Nicoletta down.

"It'll be fine," she told her young sister-in-law, with more confidence than she really felt. "The count will give his consent on the spot, and you'll be married in a month."

"It may take a little longer than that to arrange," Demetrio said. It was dinnertime, and he had just joined them.

"I think a month is quite long enough," Reva insisted, a little sharply. "I hope you'll press for an early wedding."

"Bad tactics," Demetrio said at once. "It looks eager."

Reva met his eyes. "Nonetheless . . ." she said significantly.

His eyes fell first. "Let's get through this one evening and worry about other things afterward," he said gruffly.

"But this one evening seems to me an excellent time to announce an engagement," Reva pointed out.

Demetrio shrugged. "To me, too. It's Torvini you have to persuade."

"Don't worry. I'll persuade him."

On the night of the reception, Nicoletta came to Reva's room, and they dressed together. Nicoletta's dress was a cream satin that looked lovely against her warm skin. With her hair hanging loose, she presented a charming picture of youth and beauty. Only when she was completely ready did Reva turn her attention to her own appearance.

The glorious black dress slipped onto her smoothly. It left her shoulders completely bare, then clung to her body like a second skin, dropping to her waist and flaring out over her hips to drop to the floor in a straight line. At the back it was slit to the thigh so that she could walk easily, and dance.

There was a tiny, glittering black-and-silver jacket that came to just below the armpits. Nicoletta held it up for her to slip into, and the two of them considered her reflection. "I was right when I took you to Primo," Nicoletta said with a sigh of pleasure.

"Yes," Reva said slowly. "You were right."

In fact, she was slightly stunned by the sight of herself. This was a woman she didn't know, glamorous, sophisticated, serenely composed.

There was a knock on the door, and Demetrio called, "May I come in?"

"Yes, yes," Nicoletta called excitedly.

He was in white tie and tails, a superbly handsome masculine figure. He entered the room holding the flat box that contained the diamonds. "Do we meet with your approval?" Nicoletta asked, twirling so that her dress swirled out.

"Of course you do," he said, but his eyes were fixed on Reva.

She tried to maintain her composure, but she was intensely aware of Demetrio's gaze, and the stunned look in his eyes. For once he was completely taken aback, and she couldn't help feeling a certain satisfaction. When they'd first met, things had happened so fast between them that she'd never gone through a stage of needing his approval. *And heaven knows,* she thought, *I don't need it now!* And yet there was a mysterious sweetness in knowing that she had it.

Out of the corner of her eye she saw Nicoletta tactfully vanish from the room. She was alone with Demetrio for the first time since the morning she'd awoken with a joyful consciousness of him, only to find him gone. Now she realized that she had actually missed him. Even their antagonism was preferable to the flat staleness of the days without him.

"You look—" he seemed to be struggling for words "—incredible."

"You said you wanted me to outshine every other woman in the room," she reminded him. "It was part of our bargain."

"Bargain," he said. "Yes . . . we made a bargain." He sounded dazed.

"Are those my—the estate diamonds?" she asked with a glance at the box.

"Yes." He laid the box down on her dressing table and opened it, but made no move to touch the jewels. Reva slipped off the little jacket and tentatively lifted the bracelet and laid it over her wrist. But the clasp defied her efforts to close it with one hand. She looked up at Demetrio, but he seemed reluctant to come near her. "I'll need some help," she said.

Still he didn't move. "If you sit down and lay your arm on the dressing table, you should be able to manage," he said.

She tried it, but the clasp still defeated her. "If you want me to wear these, you'll have to help me," she said.

There was no doubting the look on his face. He didn't want to touch her. For a moment she was annoyed, forgetting how firmly she'd forbidden him. But then she saw his eyes again. They were resting on her, full of awe and—something else. At last he lifted the bracelet and wrapped it around her wrist. An inner disturbance rocked Reva when she realized that his hands were shaking. He almost dropped the bracelet, and would have done so had she not seized it quickly, her fingers folding over his. For a long moment they were still, listening to the sound of each other's breathing. Then she removed her hand, and he finished fastening the bracelet.

In the mirror she saw him lift the necklace. There was a shock as the cold diamonds touched her skin, and then the sensation of his warm fingers on the back of her neck. Uncontrollable tremors went through her. She was exceptionally sensitive just there, and all down her spine. How often had he kissed the length of her back while she reveled in it? Meeting his eyes in the mirror, she saw that he, too, was remembering.

"Why did you stay away?" she whispered.

"You know why," he told her. With a visible effort, he added, "I was doing what you wanted."

She gave a little half smile. "Well, I'm sure it's the only time," she said, not unkindly, but with a wry sadness.

"No," he said seriously. "I was always trying to do what you wanted—and always getting it wrong."

"I guess we were neither of us very clever," she said with a sigh. She rose and put on the tiny jacket.

"Reva—wait," Demetrio said suddenly. "Can't we put aside our private differences for tonight—for Nicoletta's sake?"

"I thought that was what we were doing—otherwise how do I come to be here?"

"Yes, but I mean more. They'll be watching us, ready to pounce on any flaw in the performance."

"Then the performance must be flawless," she said, smiling. "Don't worry. We'll fool them all."

Nicoletta burst eagerly back into the room. "The first cars are beginning to arrive," she cried.

"We must take our places, ready to receive them," Demetrio said.

He offered her his arm. She took it, and raised her
head. Demetrio was one of the few men tall enough to
make her look up to him. "Let's go," she said.

Six

Everywhere the house seemed to have been turned into a bower of flowers. They decked the windows and doors and wreathed the banisters that led up from the great hall to the upper floor. Behind them, in the ballroom, the orchestra that had been hired for the evening was already playing softly. The three of them took their places at the top of the stairs, with Nicoletta in the center, and almost immediately the guests began to appear through the far doors, making their way across the mosaic floor and up the stairs, smiles in position.

Reva knew many of them as Demetrio's business acquaintances, some colleagues, some rivals. Even those whom she knew disliked him greeted him with respect and protestations of friendship, and she saw that they were afraid of him. They were right to be afraid, she thought. He was a hard man, a man without scruples. And yet...

She saw him turn to Nicoletta and give her an encouraging squeeze. There was a gentle, tender look on his face, as though it were with her alone that he could risk open, trusting affection. Reva remembered the many faces he had shown her during the stormy year of their marriage. She had seen him passionate, even tender, but never defenseless. Always she'd sensed that one final barrier was still in place, as if he mistrusted the power of his own feelings for her. Or mistrusted *her,* perhaps?

But with Nicoletta, the sister so much younger than himself that he treated her almost as a daughter, he felt free to give himself unreservedly. Reva gave a mental shrug. That was understandable, surely? But she couldn't quite banish a little ache about her heart at the thought of how different things might have been between them.

She came back to reality to realize that the house was overflowing with people. Most of the guests had arrived, and the buzz of conversation was rising to a soft roar. Three people were advancing across the great hall and up the stairs. In the front were a man and a woman in their late fifties. Countess Torvini was majestically attired in haute couture and adorned with emeralds. The count had once been handsome, but now his lean face was marred by a hard mouth and cynical eyes. He walked with his head high and an air of arrogance that suggested generations of aristocrats.

The steward drew a deep breath and announced the Torvini family. Reva shook hands, smiled and murmured pleasantries as Demetrio introduced her. She knew she was being sized up. It seemed she passed muster, because the countess favored her with a little smile and the count gave a brief nod of acceptance. She wished she felt as charitable toward them, but they struck her as proud, disagreeable people, and she pitied Nicoletta if she married into the family.

She wondered if she ought to be a good sister and warn her, but then Guido came into view, and an unmistakable tremor of joy went through Nicoletta. Reva felt it, and realized that her young sister-in-law was beyond reason. She was wildly in love, in the grip of a violent passion, and no words of caution would get through to her. Reva knew that feeling so well, and the bitterness to which it could lead.

Guido was amazingly handsome, with dark, beautiful eyes, perfect features, and a curved mouth. He was in his mid-twenties, and carried the air of one who had been admired all his life. He greeted Reva with charming courtesy, bowing low over her hand and murmuring a polished greeting. To Demetrio he was deferential, but when he took Nicoletta's hand, joy shone from him. They stood smiling at each other until the count said wryly, "Guido." Instantly the young man dropped Nicoletta's hand, looking apprehensive. "Yes, Papà," he muttered, and moved on.

It was time for supper. Reva smiled at the count who gallantly extended his arm for her, and she led him to the place of honor.

"May I say how delighted I am to renew our acquaintance?" he said smoothly when they were seated and the first course was being served. "Dare I hope to have been remembered?"

"I remember you very well," she said with a smile.

"How charming. I was certain that our two families would become friends, despite our very great differences. Unfortunately, you departed soon after." His eyes were bright with significance.

"I'm afraid my departure has been misunderstood," Reva said smoothly. "I left Milan temporarily because of my work. My husband has always been very understanding about my career."

"A career that takes you away from him? Truly, he must be a rare man." He gave her a smile that didn't reach his eyes. "Doubtless I seem very old-fashioned to you. I was born into a more...shall we say, 'traditional' culture, and my own dear wife has no interests outside her home and family."

"I'm sure they make her completely happy," Reva said politely.

"Totally," Torvini said, with insufferable complacency. Then he added, "I gather Nicoletta admires you very much."

Sensing danger, Reva said quickly, "Nicoletta and I are fond of each other, but that doesn't mean we're alike. She's a product of your traditional culture. All she wants is Guido for her husband, and plenty of children."

"Do women like that really exist any more?"

"Not many of them. You should make sure of her for your son while you can."

Torvini laughed. "You have sharp wits, *signora*. As for my son—well, we shall see. There's still much to be considered. In the Torvini family, marriages have never been made for pleasure alone. A marriage is an alliance between one family and another. There is such a thing as suitability—and unsuitability."

She couldn't resist saying, "In this day and age?"

He gave a chilly laugh. "Even today, alliances are formed. Perhaps not always for the same reasons, but the ties of family cement an arrangement in a way that nothing else does. But your sister-in-law is charming. Quite charming."

As he spoke, he glanced at Nicoletta, who was sitting beside Guido, smiling into his eyes. Reva felt a rush of anger at the idea that the girl's feelings should be tossed this way and that in the steel grip of this man's notions of suitability. "If they love each other, I think that should be enough," she said firmly. "She adores your son. What could be more suitable than that?"

"But how long does young love last?" Torvini asked gravely. "Without compatibility of mind and upbringing, what is left when the first passionate feeling dies?"

"In the best marriages, it doesn't die," Reva insisted. "It only mellows. And that has little to do with compatibility of mind and upbringing."

"No? Well, perhaps this is a matter in which you can instruct me. You and your husband seem to be incompatible in almost everything—country, background, expectations. But your marriage is clearly a triumphant success. You would describe it as that?"

"Surely my presence here is proof?"

He smiled. "Hardly, *signora*. You've been absent for a long time, and now you reappear at a convenient moment. A cynical man might suspect this was a farce for my benefit."

"A cynical man would probably suspect anything and everything," she responded lightly.

"True. And I don't like to think of myself as a cynic. In my own way, I'm a romantic. In this day and age, only a true romantic stands up for the old virtues of fidelity and family stability. Very well, then. You and Demetrio are living proof that a solid marriage can be welded out of great differences. I congratulate you. And I envy you your great happiness."

Reva smiled and inclined her head. There was nothing else to do. She'd come too far to back out now, but she was uneasy at the turn the conversation had taken.

Luckily, he began to make conversation with the neighbor on his other side. Reva breathed a sigh of relief. Out of the corner of her eye she saw Demetrio glancing in her direction. She looked at him and saw him make a minor adjustment to his tie. Without having to think about it, she immediately brushed her fingertips across her right cheek. Then she stopped, astounded at herself.

The movements had looked casual, but the adjustment to his tie had meant, "Is everything all right?" Her answering gesture had told him she was fine. A touch on the left cheek would have brought him over to find out what was wrong. It was a code they'd worked out in the first month of their marriage for communicating at large functions, but it was part of her past. She hadn't thought of it for a year. Her response had been instinctive and unhesitating.

Then, with a sense of cold shock, the dreadful truth dawned on her. Demetrio *had* forgotten the code. He hadn't been signaling at all, merely fiddling with his tie. Had her response recalled everything to his mind? And if so, was he feeling triumphant because she'd lost a point in their battle? To her horror she felt her cheeks growing warm and knew she was blushing. The heat radiated out until it encompassed her whole body. Hastily she slipped off the little jacket, and turned to her other neighbor, hoping her embarrassment didn't show, especially to the one man who would understand it.

Demetrio, watching her, waited for her to look back at him. When she didn't, he was forced to give his attention to Countess Torvini. But while his lips mouthed polite nothings, his mind was full of dismay. She'd understood his signal. He was sure of it. She'd responded in the old way, but then had been furious at herself for yielding to that old memory, and had turned away from him. He looked at the two little pennants of color in her cheeks that betrayed her anger. If only she would look at him again, meet his eyes, perhaps exchange a smile of remembrance. But no. She had shut him out.

He thought how magnificent she looked, with the diamonds glittering against her flawless skin. There was something about her that made every man in the room conscious of her. He'd seen it when they'd all stood in the reception line. The women had studied her in curiosity and envy, but the men's eyes had held another look—the look of the predator. There wasn't one of them who hadn't wondered about the lithe body encased in the skintight black, wondered and speculated. The thought made his brow damp. Any man here was free to envision his wife's nakedness. Only he was forbidden. She was like a queen, casting all other women into the shade, beautiful, glamorous—and remote.

Remote. His mind seized on the word as so often in the past it had seized on clues that might explain her. How could a woman who laughed and loved with such passion, who was such an eager bedmate, be called remote? And yet there had always been something about her that wasn't wholly his. He rediscovered the bitter truth now, and it was as painful as the first time.

The orchestra had started to play softly in the background. As guest of honor, the count was entitled to the first dance with his hostess, and Reva took the arm he gallantly proffered. Demetrio rose, smiling, and led the countess onto the floor. Out of the corner of her eye Reva

saw Nicoletta and Guido melt into each other's arms as
the orchestra swelled into a waltz.

Torvini danced correctly and made polite conversation, but Reva was sure she didn't have his full attention. His eyes flickered constantly around the room,
sizing up the other guests. It was a relief when their duty
dance was over.

She danced with Guido and found him delightful. His
movements were fluid and inspired, and he had a lot of
gentle charm. But Reva had the impression that he lacked
the confidence of a young man of twenty-six, which she
knew him to be. It was easy to see how he'd captured Nicoletta's heart, but in Reva's eyes he was still very im-
mature. Would it be more pleasant, she wondered, to be
married to this sweet-tempered boy than to have a husband who was uncompromising and ruthless? It seemed
that Nicoletta had instinctively chosen someone who was
the opposite of her brother, and perhaps she was wise.

Her eyes flickered to Demetrio, who was now dancing
with the wife of a fellow industrialist. He danced as he
did everything, she thought, efficiently but without
imagination. But then justice forced her to realize that
Demetrio didn't need to be an easy dancer to make an
impact on the floor. He achieved that simply by being
half a head taller than any man there, and radiating
power and confidence in a way that set him apart, like the
leader of a pride of lions. Harsh and unyielding he might
be, impossible to live with. But he was a *man*. He had
brains, vision and force, the kind on which civilizations
were built. And there wasn't another man there who
could hold a candle to him.

Next she found herself dancing with a man called
Bruno Alessi. She'd met him briefly in the reception line,
but had no idea who he was, although his name was

vaguely familiar. He was about thirty, with a weak mouth and a bitter expression. Through his politeness, Reva could sense a hostility toward her that puzzled her. The mystery was soon explained. "How do you like living in my home, Signora Corelli?" he asked.

"Your home?"

"It was once my home, before your husband hounded our family out of it."

Now she remembered where she'd heard the name Alessi before. "I—I'm sorry," she managed to say at last.

"Don't apologize. It wasn't your doing. Even the sight of my mother's diamonds about your neck doesn't make me blame you personally," he added with a half-suppressed vehemence. "Nobody can stand up against him. My father gave Demetrio Corelli his start. He loaned him money, introduced him to influential men, put business his way. But none of that counted with Demetrio when it came to getting possession of our home. What he wants, he takes—as his wife, you must know that better than anyone."

Reva's mouth tightened with annoyance. She instinctively disliked this young man, and wasn't prepared to believe him until she'd heard the other side of the story. "You can't expect me to discuss my husband with you," she said coldly.

"Of course not. I suppose you, too, are afraid of him?"

"Certainly not," she said sharply.

"Most of the people in this room are scared stiff of Demetrio Corelli. They know what it's in his power to do, and what he'd actually be *prepared* to do—not always the same thing. They know he doesn't care who he crushes."

"That's enough," she said in a hard voice. Her fury was rising. Thinking badly of her husband was her privilege. The discovery that someone else did so, and was prepared to speak his vile thoughts aloud, was intolerable.

But Alessi's hatred was apparently too great for him to heed her warning. He went on, grinding out his bitterness and spite, until Reva had a strong instinct to slap his face and storm off the dance floor. But that would cause a scandal. There had to be a subtler way.

Suddenly she stopped and swayed slightly, her hand to her head. "I'm feeling a little faint," she murmured.

Several men around her at once deserted their partners to help her to the side. As she sat down, she looked from beneath her lashes to where Bruno Alessi stood, his lips tight. He, at least, wasn't deceived about her "illness," she thought.

"Get back. *Get back.*"

The little crowd parted at the sound of the commanding voice. The next moment, Demetrio appeared on the scene. Reva's eyes were half-closed, and she was caught off guard when he lifted her bodily in his arms. He swept out of the ballroom into a little anteroom, where he kicked the door closed and set her down on a sofa. But instead of laying her back, he kept her in his arms, with her head on his shoulder. "What is it?" he demanded urgently. *"Reva!"*

His voice was shaking with some strong emotion, and the sound of it rocked her to the core. "Demetrio," she murmured, disconcerted and uncertain how she ought to act now.

"Yes, darling, what is it?" he said quickly. "What happened? Speak to me. It's not like you to faint."

"I didn't," she said reluctantly. She wondered if he realized he'd called her "darling."

"Nonsense. Of course you did. I was watching you, and I saw you collapse. Why didn't you tell me you were feeling ill?"

"But I'm not." She disengaged herself, knowing that she was heading into stormy waters but there was no help for it. "Demetrio, there is nothing wrong with me."

"You don't know that."

"But I do. I didn't faint at all. It was an act. I needed to get away, and it was the best I could think of."

She saw the disbelief in his eyes, followed immediately by belief, shock, anger. Watching him, she could chart the progress through embarrassed realization of how emotionally he'd behaved, through to the donning of a cold, ironic mask. "I see," he said, drawing back from her. "One of your little games."

"No, it wasn't a little game. He was slandering you, and if I hadn't 'fainted,' I'd have slapped his face."

If she'd expected Demetrio to be grateful, she would have been disappointed. "You should have let him slander me," he said, rising to his feet. "My back is broad."

"And that's all the thanks I get for defending you?" she said indignantly.

He grinned. "My dear wife . . . why bother?"

She sighed. "Why indeed?"

"Besides, *did* you defend me? Or did you faint to avoid having to say anything? Weren't you afraid of letting him know how much you agreed with him?"

She got up from the sofa and faced him. "As a matter of fact, I was really angry for your sake. Why, I can't imagine."

"What did he say about me?"

"That his father was kind to you, and you repaid him by stabbing him in the back and seizing his home by dubious methods."

Demetrio nodded. "Yes, that's what I imagined."

"Well?"

"Well, what?"

"Were your methods dubious?"

His eyes glinted unpleasantly. "What a question for a wife to ask her husband! Besides, you know all about my methods. You've often favored me with your opinions of my calculating, unscrupulous, ruthless— I forget the rest, but you probably remember it."

"Demetrio, don't play with me," she pleaded. "Tell me the truth."

He raised a sardonic eyebrow. "Good heavens, Reva, don't tell me you've actually gotten around to asking questions *before* you form your opinions. Of course, that's what a good journalist is supposed to do, but then, *I* was never given the benefit of the doubt, was I?"

"I'm a photojournalist. I don't deal in words."

"Except once. The pictures you took of Michael Denton were excellent, but it was what you found out and set down in words that really made your reputation, wasn't it? If I hadn't been fool enough to make it easy for you that time, you might have been a better wife."

She regarded him, her head on one side. "Now it's coming out. It's always galled you that you gave me my first big success, hasn't it?"

He grinned. "Not half as much as it's galled you, my dear. Now, shall we return to our guests?"

He gave her his arm in a gallant gesture that was half mockery, and Reva took it. Their reentry into the ballroom made a small commotion. Reva smiled and made reassuring replies to everyone who asked her if she was feeling better. Then Count Torvini descended on her, all concern. "Please," she said hastily, "it was only that I got a little too hot."

"And a little tired, I think," he said. "I'm afraid you've worn yourself out preparing this magnificent evening. You need a rest, and I know the very place. Next week my family leaves for a short holiday at our villa on Lake Como. It would make us so happy if you and your husband would join us. And Nicoletta, too, of course."

"Oh, yes, that would be wonderful," Nicoletta said eagerly. She cast an imploring glance at her brother and her sister-in-law.

Reva felt herself being gradually entangled. She didn't want this visit, which would inevitably throw her closely into Demetrio's company, but there was no way she could refuse. While she hesitated, she heard Demetrio uttering graceful words of acceptance.

The evening was coming gently to a close. Demetrio glanced at the conductor and gave him a signal. "I told him to play a final waltz," he explained to Reva. "I haven't yet danced with my wife."

As he spoke, he extended his hands toward her. Reva hesitated. She didn't want to be held in Demetrio's arms. It wasn't safe. But the farce must be played out to the end, so she smiled and allowed him to take her to the dance floor. Nicoletta watched them, smiling. Then she whispered something to a servant, and the next moment the lights were dimmed.

"Trust Nicoletta to get her own way," Demetrio said. "She wants to dance closely with Guido, and a little darkness is useful for that."

Reva didn't answer at once. The feel of his warm breath on her bare shoulder was sending tremors through her, and it was hard to talk. "What have you let us in for?" she said at last.

"It wasn't my fault. There was no way out. You saw that."

"Yes," she with a sigh. "For Nicoletta's sake."

"It's a sign of approval. You must have made a good impression on him."

"I'm not so sure. He's suspicious of my sudden reappearance. He as good as said so."

"Then the invitation is to test us further."

"This is mad," she murmured. "We can't go on like this."

"We must, for as long as we have to." He tightened the arm about her waist.

"Don't hold me so close," she whispered furiously.

"I'm merely doing my duty. Torvini is watching us, and at all costs he must be fooled. Look up at me and smile. Try to seem as if my company enchanted you."

An ironic reply hovered on her lips, and died when her eyes met his. Far back in their depths was something that wasn't mockery, something that stirred her and made her breath come fast. She couldn't go to Lake Como with Demetrio. She must get away from him quickly and try to restore the sanity he'd threatened.

"Once you could have looked enchanted without effort," he reminded her.

"That was a long time ago."

"No, it was less than two years. That's what's so sad about us. Doesn't it make you sad, Reva?"

She whispered, "Yes." She could hardly speak.

"Once we would have clung to each other in the dance, and thought ahead to when I would remove that dress and kiss every inch of your body."

"Don't," she whispered in anguish. "I can't bear it."

"What can't you bear? To be reminded that there was a time when you wanted me?"

"No, not that. It's just—that we lost it. So much feeling, so much happiness. And it all counted for nothing in the end."

"I don't believe that. Once we loved each other, and love must always count for something."

"It wasn't love, or it wouldn't have died so soon. We both know what really united us, Demetrio. And it doesn't last."

"Doesn't it? Have you really forgotten how it was between us, how it felt to give and take pleasure all night? Since you left, there's been no other woman in my bed. There's nobody else I want. You've destroyed all other women for me. Does that make you glad?"

"Stop this," she said fiercely. "Let the past die."

"The past can never be dead when the feel of you in my arms makes me forget everything else."

"Then open your arms and let me go."

"Not until the dance is over. Until then, we're condemned to stay together, and endure each other as best we can. I told you there had been no other woman." When she didn't answer, he tightened his grip on her. *"Tell me."*

"I've lived as though we were still married," she conceded.

"We *are* still married. That hasn't changed."

"And you haven't changed, either," she said angrily. His words and his closeness were sending tremors of terrifying pleasure through her. "You're as unscrupulous as you ever were. You promised me that this wouldn't happen."

"I promised not to try to sleep with you, and I'll keep my word. But nothing in our bargain prohibits me from saying anything I want, and at this moment I want to remind you of the truths you prefer to forget."

"Truth?" She flung the word at him. "To you, truth is just another weapon."

"Right now it's the best weapon I have. You and I found ecstasy in each other's arms. That's the truth. And ecstasy, once found, can't be forgotten. It haunts you and mocks your attempts to deny it. It makes every moment dangerous. We can't meet without remembering how we can make each other feel. We can't hate without recognizing how flimsy hate is, and how easily passion can burn it up. These are truths, and you know it. If they weren't truths, you wouldn't be so frightened of them."

"I'm not afraid," she told him challengingly.

"If you're not afraid, prove it by inviting me to your room tonight."

"You devil," she whispered. "Let me go at once."

"And make everybody talk? Don't you understand that while the music's playing we're both prisoners?"

He could have bitten his tongue the moment he uttered the fatal word *prisoners*. In despair he saw her face close against him at the hated memory. "Reva..." he said.

But the music was coming to an end. She drew herself out of his arms and turned quickly away.

Seven

The house was dark and quiet. The last guest had departed. Reva had gone to bed immediately, and a moment later Nicoletta had danced blissfully down the corridor to her room, humming as she went. After a brief silence, Reva had heard Demetrio go into his own room next door.

She undressed mechanically. The evening was replaying in her head, the lights, the music, Demetrio's arms about her, his hot eyes on her. The replay came to an end and immediately started again. Her mind couldn't free itself from that endless repetition. It was caught up, wondering, persuading, incredulous of its own thoughts.

She'd set all her will and determination against Demetrio's evocation of the past, but she'd gained only an outward victory. Inwardly she was in turmoil. He'd used every trick he knew to ignite memories of their passionate nights together, reminding her with words, with touch, and with the overwhelming impact of his physical nearness. Now those nights lived again for her, as vivid and searing as if it were only yesterday, and her body responded helplessly to the echoes of the old magic.

She discovered that she'd showered and put on her nightdress and negligee. She had no memory of doing so, or of replacing the fabulous diamonds in their box. They lay there glittering fiercely against the black velvet. Her mind, working on its own track, which seemed to be independent of her will, insisted that it wasn't safe to keep the diamonds here. They were worth a king's ransom, and must be returned to Demetrio tonight, this instant.

She took out the key to the connecting door and stood, hesitating, before turning it. The latch slipped back easily. She tried the handle, wondering if the door would turn out to be bolted from the other side, but it gave under her hand, and she pushed it slightly open. From the little bathroom came sounds that meant Demetrio was having a shower. Reva stepped quietly into the room and stood still, her heart hammering. Even now it wasn't too late to turn back, but something seemed to have taken her over, making her do things she hadn't meant to do. It made her turn off the bedside light so that the room was dark except for the moonlight that came in through the tall windows.

She heard the sound of running water cease, and a moment later the bathroom door opened. She sensed rather than saw Demetrio halt on the threshold. Then his voice broke the silence. "Who's there? Who is that?"

On impulse she said, "My name doesn't matter."

He put up his hand to the light switch on the wall, but she brushed against him in the semidarkness, whispering, "Don't do that. It's better as it is."

"Why are you here?" He sounded cautious, not himself.

"I thought you wanted me here. At least— Perhaps it was some other woman you were hoping for. Shall I go?"

"No," he said slowly. "As you said, names don't matter. Nothing matters except that—you're here."

"Didn't you know I would be?" she asked, coming close to him. She couldn't see his face, but she could sense the trembling of his body.

"I wasn't sure," he said. "I hoped—but then, I've hoped for so many things, and been disappointed."

In the silence that followed, she put up a hand and gently touched his cheek. He drew a sudden sharp breath. "Perhaps you should have more faith?" she murmured. As she spoke, she let her hand trail down the length of his neck. Then she pushed the silk robe so that it fell from his shoulders, leaving him naked.

Still he didn't touch her. He seemed afraid to. "I watched you all evening," he said. "You were the most beautiful woman in the room. Every man there wanted you, and I could tell you were laughing at them all."

"*All* of them?" she asked significantly.

"Yes, *all*. You watched them making fools of themselves over you, and you laughed. I know you."

"No," she said quickly. "You don't know me, and I don't know you. We never met before tonight."

With his fingertips he left a trail of fire down her breasts. The sensation felt so good that she almost groaned aloud. "We met a million years ago," he said huskily.

"A million years," she agreed. "A thousand million years." She slipped her robe off, letting him see her glorious nakedness in the moonlight. "And yet tonight we meet as strangers. We never saw each other before, and maybe we'll never see each other again. There's only this one night . . . no questions . . ."

"No questions," he echoed, taking her into his arms.

The sensation of his body against hers was like coming home. For a few frantic minutes, they touched each other everywhere, in urgent rediscovery. He was familiar but different, harder, leaner, but with the same electric energy, the same thrilling strength and vigor. "Who are you?" he murmured as he kissed her face, her neck, her hair. *"Who are you?"*

"I'm the woman you were waiting for," she whispered. "And you're the man I came to find. Nothing else matters."

"But tomorrow—"

"Hush." She laid soft fingers over his lips. "Tomorrow doesn't exist."

He seized her hand and buried his lips in the palm. His hot breath sent shivers of pleasure through her. His free arm was holding her tightly against him, and she could feel the steely thigh muscles and the hot urgency of his aroused manhood pressed against her. Reva's heart was racing. However this had come about, now that it had started, she knew there was no turning back. She wanted Demetrio, and for tonight she didn't care what she had to do to have him. Tomorrow it would be different. But tomorrow they would be other people.

She ran her fingers through his dark, springy hair, pulling his head around so that she could lock her mouth on his and invade him with her tongue. His own tongue immediately challenged her in return, thrusting deeply into her mouth, rediscovering the soft skin that he'd once loved to caress, skin that was eager for him now.

She ran her hands over as much of his body as she could reach. He was as magnificent as ever, broad-shouldered, lean-hipped, with heavy, muscular thighs. How had she ever imagined that she could live in the same house with him and not desire him to the point of madness? She could face the truth now. She'd been fighting her growing passion since the moment he'd stepped into her room in Milan, and now it was beyond her control. She wanted him with a raw, basic hunger that would brook no refusal. And he wanted her. As always in the past, the knowledge of his desire excited her own still further. By day, nothing had changed. Their personalities clashed as sharply as ever. But here there were no personalities, only naked flesh, the thrilling scents of arousal in man and woman, and the sweet, hot darkness where the world stopped for them.

He stooped and put an arm beneath her knees, lifting her high. Reva turned slightly in his arms so that her breasts lay against his chest and she could feel the thundering of his heart. Her own heart was pounding to the same thrilling rhythm as he lowered her onto the bed and began kissing her madly on her face, her neck, her breasts. She groaned with pleasure and offered herself to his caresses, caressing him back, wanting him everywhere at once.

She felt his mouth encompass one hard, peaked nipple. His tongue began teasing it this way and that, each rasping movement sending tremors of pleasure scurrying through her body to her fingers and toes. Every inch of her had come newly alive, burning and vibrant, making her realize that the peace she'd thought she had this past year had been nothing more than the apathy of the half-dead. Without his touch, her flesh had lain sullen and cold, and she'd deluded herself into believing that was peace.

There had never been peace in her relationship with Demetrio. There never could be. That wasn't the kind of people they were. Both of them hot-tempered and vigorous, they'd confronted each other in a battle for supremacy to which there could be no end, only the occasional armed truce.

Her lips framed his name, but she wouldn't utter it aloud. They were strangers, meeting on the simple plane of raw lust, where no questions need be asked. It was the only way tonight could work.

But she couldn't stop herself breathing a long, urgent *"Please."* He responded at once, moving between her legs and thrusting into her without delay. She encompassed him eagerly, groaning with satisfaction as she felt the hardness come deep within her to reach the very wellspring of passion. He seemed to be made of steel, fine-sprung, tireless, powerful enough to thrust and thrust again with his lean, muscular hips.

The pleasure was indescribable. She thrust back at him with strong, purposeful movements, increasing the friction that was sending her half-crazy with delight. He'd always loved the fact that she was an active lover, engaging him in sensual battle. And she'd always loved the fact that he could cope with her erotic aggression. He could take whatever challenge she threw at him, and challenge her in turn. The arrogance that infuriated her by day translated at night into a self-confidence that gave her freedom. And again she had the thought that had occurred to her at the reception. Whatever else he might be, he was a *man*.

She'd endured a year without the physical fulfillment only Demetrio could give her, and now she needed it. She devoured him with lips and hands and loins. All her memories came rushing back. She knew where and how he liked to be touched, knew the words he enjoyed hearing whispered in his ear. She knew the things that enchanted him, the things that incited him. She knew what drove him wild.

She groaned aloud as she felt her climax approaching, and then she was exploding inside with pleasure heightened to a pitch of blinding intensity, pleasure that streamed through her in dazzling cascades of light and heat, right out to her fingers and toes, yet seemed at the same time to stay concentrated in her burning loins.

It was over, and yet it had only just started. He was still hard inside her, starting to move again, slowly, and she remembered his awesome strength. Many nights he'd pleased her until the dawn, slept an hour, then gone to work with undiminished energy. She clasped him to her. His body was like steel, the back muscles tensing and relaxing easily as he drove into her and then withdrew, in long leisurely movements. She enjoyed it best this way, with time to savor every tiny feeling.

She began to rock her hips in rhythm with his controlled movements. The intensity of each drawn-out sensation was a mind-blowing experience. She'd known such keen pleasure before with Demetrio, but after a year's deprivation she came to it with a new hunger.

Primo had been right about her. She was a woman of the world, a woman of experience whose eroticism matched Demetrio's perfectly. Whatever he did in bed had the touch of danger. Everything about his lean, hard body, the narrow hips and loins, with their barely leashed power, the arms that could encircle a woman in a hold that was gentle but as unbreakable as iron, everything was suffused with danger. Some women would have found that intimidating, but to Reva it was wildly exciting. To her, life was nothing without adventure, and that was as true of sex as of everything else.

She didn't think of what they were doing now as making love. How could it be, when they'd agreed to be strangers? This was simply sex—wild, uninhibited, utterly enjoyable sex, an encounter with a perfect male body that possessed incredible sensual skills, sex with no strings, no questions, no arguments, no consequences. It was wonderful.

The pleasure was beginning to mount again, but it was too soon. She wanted more time to enjoy this blissful physical state. "No," she gasped. "Not yet."

He slowed, thrusting less deeply, hard enough to continue sending exquisite vibrations through her, but holding himself back for her sake. "Is that how you like it?" he growled.

And she answered, as she'd so often answered in the past, "Yes . . . like that . . . just like that . . ."

She was possessed by sheer mindless ecstasy. It convulsed her body, making her head toss and her hair splay out on the pillow. She was dimly aware of his face, looking down at her as she writhed in an erotic frenzy. He was smiling, and his eyes glittered as he drove her on to greater heights.

"Now?" he asked at last.

"Yes," she breathed. "Yes—*now*."

This time she was ready to climb to the stars with him. As his speed and power increased, she arched her back, utterly possessed by the physical sensations that blotted out everything else. Nothing had changed. After a year apart, they were still perfectly matched. They reached the final moment together, clinging to each other as though the world had dissolved into mist around them and there was nothing else to hold.

Reva lay for a moment, catching her breath, before propping herself up on one arm to look down on him. He was regarding her warily. She laughed and began to trail her fingers over his chest, tracing light patterns, silently asking if the stranger liked to be teased like this, as Demetrio always had.

Apparently he did, for he relaxed and began to take long-drawn-out breaths, letting her have her way. She drew her fingertips this way and that on his chest before making her way slowly down to his flat stomach and his narrow hips. Despite his recent exertions, he was already aroused again. Reva eyed him with eager, expectant eyes, and let her fingers enfold him tantalizingly.

He didn't speak, but his hand tightened on her shoulder, urging her in his direction. It was something he'd done often in the past, and this time there could be no doubting the signal. Reva moved over him swiftly. Her independent nature loved this part, when she could use her imagination to tease him, and the strength of her loins and thighs to thrill him. She had a subtle, flexible body that would do whatever she asked of it. She rocked back and forth, tightening and loosening her grip on him until he groaned at the pleasure. When she paused, he regarded her sardonically. "Get tired already?"

"Like hell!" she said, and resumed her movements. "You'll tire before I will."

He nearly said, "I never have before," but remembered in time that there had been no "before." She was wise, he thought. Where there was no past, there could be no bitterness.

The next moment he lost all capacity for thought. Every nerve in his body was swamped by the sensations she was evoking in him. He reached out to settle his hands on her hips, relishing the feeling of them tensing and relaxing against his palms. Erotic power vibrated through her slight frame, belying her delicate appearance. In the darkness he could just make out her smile of triumph, and he grinned back in agreement.

It was she who decided their moment. He yielded readily to her expertise, enjoying the sensation that he was in the hands of a woman who knew exactly what she was doing. When they had exploded in mutual satisfaction, she collapsed onto him, her hair flowing over his chest. He held on to her. "Enough?" he asked.

"I was going to ask you the same question," she said.

"For the moment," he answered. "There's always later."

"Greedy, huh?"

"I just like to make the most of a good thing. And you're the best thing that's come my way for—for a year."

"What would your wife do if she could hear you say that?"

He grinned in the darkness. "Well, if you don't tell her, I won't."

The next moment he knew she'd fallen asleep on his chest. She stayed in that position, sleeping as still and quiet as a child, for an hour. But then they both awoke, refreshed, and returned, laughing, to the fray.

Demetrio opened his eyes to find the soft gray light of dawn on his face. He yawned and stretched, wondering at his sense of well-being. Then he remembered.

Slowly he rose from the bed and began to look around the room. There was no definite sign that anybody else had been here, but the air still carried the indefinable trace of her subtle perfume, and the bed was in total disarray, as if a battle royal had been fought on it. His silk robe lay on the floor where it had fallen.

He tried the connecting door and found it locked. Beside it, on the dresser, lay the flat black box with the diamonds.

Eight

Two days before they were due to leave for Lake Como, Reva had a call from Benno Andrese asking her to come out and take some shots of another apartment. "They pay their rent to the same front company as the people in Paradise House," he explained.

Reva went and found this place even worse than the first. Benno told her he was still working on unraveling the skein that led back to the owner. "But someone knows what I'm doing," he said. "Public records that ought to be available go missing suddenly. Phones get cut off. You'd better be careful, too."

"Don't worry about me," she said blithely.

But on the way home she noticed a car in the rearview mirror. It stuck doggedly behind her, always keeping the same distance, until, on a lonely stretch of road, it put on a sudden burst of speed and drew alongside, uncomfortably close. She glanced sideways and saw that the driver was looking at her. He had a cold, hawklike face that made her shiver. With grim determination she put her foot on the gas and shot ahead. Soon she'd left the other car behind, and in a few minutes more she was home. As she turned in through the gates, her mirror showed the other car veering away out of sight. She told herself the whole thing had probably been her imagination. But if not, whoever had chased her now knew where she lived. Perhaps it was fortunate that she was going away.

Then she hurried into the house, to be greeted by Nicoletta, who was in a frenzy of excitement over her preparations, and she forgot all about it.

On the morning of their departure, the entire world seemed to go mad. When the car was loaded with their baggage and they were ready to get in, an embarrassed servant came to inform Demetrio that the main gate was locked, only someone called Toni knew where the key was, and Toni was blind drunk. It gave Reva a glimpse of another facet of her husband. Instead of being furious, he merely said, "Again?" in a voice of exasperated resignation.

"Does that mean we're trapped inside the grounds until he sobers up?" she asked.

"No, there's another gate at the rear," Demetrio said.

"Won't Toni have that key, too?"

To her surprise, Demetrio looked awkward. "Just leave me to worry about that," he said tersely. He got behind the wheel. "Hurry up and get started."

He followed a winding road that had been allowed to become overgrown. After about a mile, Reva saw a cluster of cottages. They were obviously empty, some were in disrepair. Only one seemed in good shape, and that stood with its shutters closed. "That used to be our home,"

Nicoletta said. "Demetrio, stop the car so that I can show Reva where we were born."

But Demetrio picked up speed. "There's no time," he said gruffly.

"Just a few moments..." Nicoletta pleaded.

"Do you want to make a bad impression on the Torvinis by arriving late?" he growled.

"But just—"

Demetrio exploded. *"Maria Vergine! Will you let it drop?"*

It was so unheard of for him to address his sister roughly that the two women stared at each other. Then a change came over Nicoletta's face, as if she were mentally saying, "Oh, yes, of course..." But when Reva raised quizzical eyes, Nicoletta only smiled.

A moment later they reached the rear exit. Demetrio got out and unlocked the gate with a key on his chain. When he returned to the car, he was smiling. He winked at Nicoletta and turned on the car radio. The incident was past. But there was something strange about it, and it lingered in Reva's mind.

The Torvini villa on Lake Como was about three hours' drive from Milan. Halfway there, they stopped for fuel. While Demetrio was paying, the two women stretched their legs, and Reva took the opportunity to ask, "What was all that about the cottage?"

"Nothing," Nicoletta said hastily. "It's just that we were already late. I should have thought."

"No, it's more than that. You know why Demetrio didn't want me to see his home. Why don't you tell me?"

"It's nothing—nothing at all. Look, Demetrio is signaling us that he's ready. We must hurry."

She went quickly back to the car, and Reva had no choice but to follow. But on the journey the answer came to her. The cottage was a private, special place to Demetrio, and he didn't want to share it with her. Nicoletta had realized that and was trying to spare Reva's feelings. He couldn't have told her more clearly that what had happened after the reception had been, as they'd pretended, an encounter between strangers—two bodies that had been attracted, mated and parted, without emotional involvement on either side. It had been her own idea, and yet his complete acceptance of it left her with an emptiness where her heart should have been.

They reached the lake in the late afternoon. It was about forty miles long, shaped like an inverted Y, and they drove up one of the "arms," past the point where the two joined, and on to a little village on the eastern shore.

"I'm so longing to see the villa," Nicoletta confided. Then she added a little self-consciously, "It's very famous for its architecture and art treasures."

Reva gave her a glance of sly mischief. She could see Demetrio's face in the rearview mirror. He was grinning at the same thought as she. Nicoletta couldn't care less about architecture. She saw the villa as a future home. Reva met his eyes in the mirror, and they laughed together. The emptiness vanished. There were still places where they could meet.

The next moment they were heading straight for the villa, which reared up ahead, situated on a hill. Reva gasped at the sight of the dual stairways that zigzagged up the hill, decorated with carved stone balustrades.

The entire Torvini family was there to greet them, including not only the count and countess and Guido, but also a cardinal, a bishop and a cabinet minister. Inside the house there were other guests to meet. The count explained that every summer he invited a few friends to join him at what he called his "little holiday home." Reva relaxed, thinking that the presence of a crowd would make everything easier.

A footman took her bags, and she followed him up a magnificent flight of marble stairs. Above her the ceiling soared, covered with mythical figures floating among clouds. Paintings lined the walls of the corridors, and in every corner, every alcove, stood plinths on which rested porcelain pieces of great beauty and splendor.

At last they came to a pair of cream-and-gilt doors, and the footman threw them open. He set down Reva's bags inside, bowed and departed. Reva surveyed her surroundings with pleasure. The furnishings were old-fashioned, with walnut wardrobes and a walnut head to the huge bed, but the wood was polished to a high gloss, and the atmosphere was luxurious.

The windows led onto a stone balcony that looked out directly over the lake. Sunset was bathing the deep blue water in a mellow glow. On the far side of the lake rose hills, and beyond them mountains so high that they were tipped with snow, although it was summer. Reva stood entranced at the sight of so much beauty.

She turned at a sound behind her and found Demetrio standing there. Over his shoulder she could see a man carrying his bags into the room. "We should have anticipated this," he said quickly, before she could speak. He turned away and said a word to the servant, who inclined his head and departed.

"They've given us the same room," she breathed. "I never thought of that."

"Neither did I. I swear I didn't plan this. The Torvinis simply took it for granted, and what can we say?"

"Nothing."

"There's plenty of room for us both. We need not get in each other's way."

His manner was completely impersonal, and that should have been a relief to her. But she wondered how he could be alone with her in a bedroom and not recall the other night, when they'd taken each other in a torrent of desire. There was no consciousness of it in his manner.

At dinner she found herself placed next to Cardinal Torvini, and braced herself for a searching interrogation about her marriage. But the cardinal entertained her by telling some of the funniest stories she'd ever heard, and the dinner passed merrily.

Afterward, as they all drank coffee on the balcony, overlooking the lake, an elderly man with gleaming white flowing hair came and stood beside her at the railing. "I've been hoping for the chance to apologize to you for my son's rudeness," he said.

"Your son?"

"I am Paulo Alessi. I should have been at your reception, but I was prevented. My son went, however, and I regret that he did so. His temper is unreliable."

"Please don't apologize," Reva said, warming to his courtly manners. "It must have been hard for him, seeing us in his old home."

Paulo Alessi shook his mane of snowy hair. "It hasn't been a home to Bruno since he stormed out years ago to live his own life. Since then, the only times I've ever seen him are when he wanted money. Gradually I sold off all I had to pay his debts, until only the house and certain family jewels were left. I knew he was waiting for me to die so that he could sell those, too. You understand, *signora,* it's painful to me to speak of my son like this. But

I must free your mind of any inaccuracies he may have put there."

"He told me you gave my husband a start," Reva said.

"I loaned him some money, years ago, which he's since paid back with interest. He can be a brutal operator, but he's scrupulously honest. But you know that, of course."

Reva nodded mechanically, feeling the sense of strain she always felt whenever someone assumed she knew everything about Demetrio. It was being brought home to her how little she'd ever bothered to find out, and she felt uncomfortable at the thought.

"Demetrio loaned me money on the villa," Alessi continued. "When I couldn't repay it, he offered to write off the debt in return for his mother's cottage."

"Just the cottage?" Reva asked, startled.

"It was all he wanted. He knew Bruno would bring the property developers in and demolish everything, and he wanted to prevent it. We had a long talk, and I suggested he take the whole place off my hands."

Reva stared. "It was *your* idea?"

"Oh, yes. It had become a burden I was glad to be rid of. He gave me a good price, but there wasn't much left when I'd paid off all Bruno's debts. I used it to buy myself an annuity, which keeps me very comfortable now. I don't know a lot about money, I'm afraid, but Demetrio managed everything so that Bruno can't touch any more. It gives me peace of mind, but it makes my son very angry."

"So that was it," Reva breathed.

"Of course, I don't need to defend your husband to you, of all people," Paulo continued, "but I wanted you to know the facts. I thought his sense of delicacy might have prevented him telling you everything about me."

"My husband can still surprise me," Reva said with an effort. "I hadn't really associated him with a sense of delicacy."

"He keeps it hidden from his business contacts, of course," Paulo said with a charming smile. "The worse they think of him, the better."

He looked around to answer a question from his hostess, unaware of having turned a knife in Reva's heart. Of course Demetrio kept this side of him from his business rivals, but he'd also kept it from his wife. She felt as if a door had slammed in her face, shutting her out, in company with everyone else he didn't trust.

She was thoughtful as she climbed the stairs to bed that night. Demetrio was still below, enjoying a brandy with some of the other men. She prepared for bed, listening all the while for the sound of his footsteps. When she'd showered, she'd taken up her favorite perfume and dabbed on just a little. Her mind seemed to have become detached from her body, and her eyes looked back from the mirror at a woman in a seductive nightdress, putting on a musky perfume. She didn't admit to herself what she was doing or why, but the mind sitting behind those eyes knew that this woman was making herself perfect for her lover. It laughed at her for the pretenses she still needed to keep in place, but the laughter was kindly, understanding.

The woman in the mirror seemed to be surrounded by a golden glow of anticipation as she waited for this one man. To Reva it was like watching herself moving through a dream.

And suddenly an echo started in her heart. A dream…only a dream… A voice had said, "You're only dreaming." It had been Demetrio's voice, whispering in her ear while she slept. Pleasure suffused her body. Only a dream? She'd awoken the next morning pervaded by the well-being that only he could give her. Only a dream?

She smiled to herself. She knew so many things now, including why he'd vanished the next morning. He'd been afraid of his own passion for her, and he'd fled. But there was no fleeing now. Soon he would come to her, and passion would begin again.

She got into bed, turned off the bedside light and lay there listening for Demetrio. Perhaps it would be the same as the other night—strangers in the dark. Or perhaps tonight they could meet as their real selves, and when they'd rediscovered each other physically they might talk quietly and let their hearts become reacquainted. She was beginning to understand that there were long, interesting vistas in her husband's nature, and that he was a more fascinating man than she had ever dreamed.

She awoke with a start and realized that the dawn light had begun to creep between the cracks of the shutters. The bedside clock showed her that she'd slept for four hours. The other side of the bed was flat and cold.

Slipping out of bed, she pulled on a negligee and opened the shutters slightly. From below she could just hear Demetrio engaged in conversation with Count Torvini. He sounded completely absorbed. Reva went back to bed and pulled the clothes over her head. It was better than throwing something, which was what she wanted to do.

Once she'd settled in at the villa, Reva found that she was enjoying herself far more than she'd expected to. The lake was a playground where it was possible to swim, laze in the sun or go out in a boat. Moreover, the luxurious villas that rose from the shore were holiday homes to much of Italian high society, and there were constant comings and goings among friends. There were several days when, what with her shopping and sightseeing expeditions with some of the other women, Demetrio's fishing trips with Paulo Alessi and a round of evening parties, she hardly saw her husband.

Count Torvini's own party for the neighborhood was a fancy-dress ball. Demetrio refused even to consider dressing up, but Reva chose a version of a peasant dress, with a tight-waisted, heavily embroidered, swirling skirt and an off-the-shoulder blouse. The evening was a triumph from the first moment. The food and music were of the best, and the entertainment was a group of dancers who whirled and stamped to the rhythm of guitars and tambourines, spurred on by wild enthusiasm from the spectators.

After the performance, the dancers moved among the guests inviting them onto the floor. The leader of the troupe stopped in front of Reva and held out his hands. Laughing, she accepted. She was a fairly good dancer whose moderate talents had been nurtured in a dancing school in childhood, and she knew she could give a good account of herself.

In fact, she did far better than that. In moments, the other guests had stopped to watch her bending and swaying to the wild rhythms. Everything seemed to come naturally to her, and when she'd finished there was noisy applause. Her partner bent over her hands to kiss them.

Even after the last of the party guests had departed, the Torvinis and their houseguests didn't want her to stop. She clicked her fingers and danced, first with Guido, then with Paulo Alessi, until she was breathless. Demetrio didn't offer to dance with her, but he never took his eyes from her slim, graceful form as it moved this way and that. She was still dancing and skipping when she went upstairs with Demetrio.

"You've had too much champagne," he said when he'd closed the bedroom door behind them.

"I've hardly had any champagne," she complained. "I couldn't find the time between dances." She swayed gracefully about the room, then sat down suddenly on the bed and eased her shoes gingerly off her feet. "I enjoyed that, but my squashed toes will make me pay for it in the morning."

"You're very talented," Demetrio said. "There's no end to your surprises."

"My mother wanted me to become a dancer. From the time I was five I went to dancing lessons twice a week, until I got into a full-time dancing school." She gave a wry laugh. "I wasn't really up to their standard, but the head of the school was an old flame of Mum's, and he stretched a point for her. She was thrilled. I wasn't."

"Didn't you want to be a dancer?" he asked.

"No, I certainly didn't," she said, making a face. "All that stern discipline bored me rigid. You have to be really dedicated to cope with it, and I wasn't. I was living Mum's dreams, not my own."

"Didn't you ever tell her how you felt?" Demetrio asked curiously.

"I tried, but I couldn't make her listen. She'd been a dancer herself, and she'd set her heart on me having the career she'd lost when she got pregnant and had to get married. And then my father died while I was very young, and there was no money. She took three jobs to earn enough to give me my chance. It wore her out, but she kept going, because she had this vision of me bowing to the applause." Reva gave a little laugh that had more sadness in it than mirth. Painful memories were coming back to her.

"Go on," Demetrio said urgently.

She shrugged. "Surely I've told you this before."

"Not all of it. I knew you trained as a dancer and your mother encouraged you, but not the rest."

"She didn't encourage me," Reva said, with a touch of remembered resentment. "She laid all the hopes and dreams of her life on me, and they were too heavy. When I was fourteen, I broke down. I just started crying in class one day and couldn't stop. The school told her I was never going to be a first-rate dancer anyway, and I left."

"Did she blame you?" When she didn't answer, he looked at her closely and found her staring into space. "Reva," he said gently.

She seemed to come out of a trance. "My mother didn't say anything," she said. "She just seemed to lose interest in me. She died three years later. Officially it was a heart attack, but I knew the truth. She'd lost her reason to live." Reva's eyes were blank for a moment, but then she rallied and said brightly, "You'll never guess what the school careers officer wanted me to do."

"What?"

"Enlist in the army. I told her nothing in the world would ever again make me live a regimented life, one where I was continually taking orders. I got a job being an assistant in a photographer's studio, because no two days were the same, and I loved it. Discovering that I could take decent pictures was almost incidental. You're right. I never talked about this. I haven't thought about it for years. I wouldn't let myself."

"I'm not surprised," Demetrio said gently. "It must have been hurtful for you to feel that you'd failed your mother and contributed to her death."

"It is," Reva admitted. "But there's not just the hurt, there's the anger, as well. I can't help resenting her for *making* me feel that way, for making me feel a failure because I wasn't like her. There's no burden as heavy as someone else's expectations, and I swore I wouldn't carry it again if I lived to be a hundred."

Demetrio looked at her curiously. She'd never before said anything that shed so strong a light on her own character, on her life as a woman and a wife. Yet she seemed oblivious of it.

If only he'd known before, he thought. He might have been more understanding of her wandering nature, seeing it only as the result of an unlucky upbringing, and not as a rejection of him.

You could have known, said his conscience. She might have opened her heart a long time ago if you'd encouraged her to, instead of always admiring her beauty and her sexual fascination. You adored the woman, but there was a hurt little girl hiding away in there, too.

Reva padded over to the open window in her bare feet. She stood for a moment, letting the cool air play over her bare shoulders. She'd been weary a moment ago, but now she was wakeful again, alert to the beauty of the stars in the black-velvet heavens, to the silent bulk of the mountains rising beyond the lake, to every subtle change in the atmosphere. Above all, she was alert to Demetrio, who came to stand beside her on the balcony.

The lights were still on in the garden. By their soft glow they could make out the figure of Nicoletta descending the stone steps on winged feet. As she reached the bottom, a man appeared from the shadows and clasped her in his arms. The two of them stood there for a long time, motionless. There was something almost magical about such perfect stillness, as though their finding each other had answered all questions.

"She's so happy now," Reva said softly, "and she thinks it will last forever."

"Perhaps they have some secret that we lacked," Demetrio suggested.

At last Nicoletta moved, throwing back her head in an ecstatic gesture. Guido caressed her face reverently, worshipfully, before laying his lips on hers. Reva sighed. "We shouldn't really look at them."

"This isn't meant for us," Demetrio agreed. But neither of them turned away. It was as though the spell of the young people's love had reached up and transfixed them both.

"They go into each other's arms as though they'd reached the end of a journey," Demetrio said quietly. "Do you remember, Reva, how that felt?"

"No," she said thoughtfully after a moment. "It was never like that with me. To me it was like starting a journey, with no idea where the road led. I remember thinking how wonderfully exciting that was. I preferred a mystery to certainty."

"With me it was the opposite," he said. "I wanted to find my eternal home in your arms. It was a long time before I understood that words like 'eternal' made you uneasy. And I've only just this minute realized why they do."

She looked at him curiously. "You never told me you felt like that."

"You never asked," he said simply. "I'm not blaming you. We neither of us asked many questions."

"It never seemed necessary," she reflected. "Our lo— What happened between us was so instantaneous and total that...I never felt there were any unanswered questions.''

Demetrio nodded. ''Neither did I, in the beginning,'' he said. He had apparently not noticed her slip. ''It was only later...'' He let the implication hang in the air.

She sighed. ''Yes.''

''I knew something was wrong,'' he said, speaking with difficulty, for this kind of conversation came very hard to him. ''But I didn't know what to do about it. I'm not a—''

''Not a sentimental man,'' she said, a slight teasing inflection in her voice.

''I was going to say, not a subtle man. If I were, I might have been a better husband.''

''You were no worse a husband than I was a wife. Neither of us had any idea how to be married, only how to be lovers. It all happened too fast. We never gave ourselves time.''

''We have all the time we need now,'' he said softly.

''It's too late,'' she said regretfully. ''We've built up so much bitterness and anger. There are things we can't forget.''

''We can forget them for a little while,'' he said. As he spoke, he pulled at the strings that fastened her off-the-shoulder blouse in the center, making them fall open. His eyes were on her face, watching for any sign of rejection. When he saw none, he lightly touched the soft white material, drawing it down over her shoulders, then down farther, to her waist, revealing her bare breasts. The hard peaks of the nipples dispelled his last fears. Slowly he drew her against him.

Nine

This time they were not strangers, but rather a man and a woman who knew each other's bodies intimately, yet were still eager to know more. Demetrio laid his fingertips lightly against Reva's neck and gradually drew them down until they trailed over her breasts. Her breathing slowed as she absorbed the sensations of delight that his softest touch could evoke.

"Reva..." His voice was almost a whisper. "Tell me that you want me."

"Don't you know it?" she murmured in a dazed voice.

"I need to hear you say it."

"I want you, Demetrio."

"Make me believe it. Prove it to me."

She smiled and began to open the buttons of his shirt. He watched her with brooding eyes until she pulled the edges apart and laid her lips against his chest. Then he ran the fingers of one hand through her hair, tousling it, while he pulled her closer to him. She felt the groan of pleasure go through him at what her lips were doing. He wrenched off his shirt, and when she looked up she found him gazing down at her, his face dark, his broad chest rising and falling.

In a moment she was gathered in his arms, his mouth on hers, his lips moving purposefully, urging hers to open. She welcomed him gladly. This wasn't the frantic coupling of the first time. It was a heartfelt meeting. She'd wanted Demetrio's body. Now she wanted Demetrio. She could tell it was the same with him, because his tongue explored her tentatively at first, the tip flickering gently against the soft inner skin of her mouth. The very lightness of touch was a delight. Little scurries of enjoyment went through her as she answered him with her own teasing tongue.

She drew back and pulled off the remainder of her clothes. She wanted to be naked with him. When he'd tossed aside his own clothes, she took his hand and drew him toward the bed. They lay down together, holding each other close, kissing and exchanging the warmth of their flesh. Reva sighed as she felt him begin to kiss her from head to foot. She knew from experience that it could take a long time, and that when it was over she would be glowing with pleasure and expectation. She relaxed, smiling, as she felt all the old happiness being given back to her.

He took his time, putting all his skill and control at her service. As he began to trail his lips and tongue down the silky skin of her thighs, she could see that he was ready for her, but he seemed unhurried. While his mouth worked marvels, his hands were also subtly busy, caressing and stroking, teasing and exciting her with delicate touches until the whole surface of her skin was heated with eager desire.

"Demetrio..." She murmured his name on a long, languorous note that was half pleading, half possessive. There was joy in repeating that beloved name and reflecting that he was all hers. Only now did she realize the size of the risk she'd taken by leaving him, by abandoning these riches to the predatory eyes of other women. But he'd been faithful to her, as she had to him, because, even when they were hostile, they belonged to each other.

He heard her sigh his name and slipped between her legs. His entry was a leisurely, deliberate savoring of joy. She pulled him close, enfolding him lovingly in her arms as they moved together slowly. Their eyes met, and they smiled at each other. This was different from the last time they'd lain together, a few nights before. That had been a purely physical experience that had slaked her body's thirst but left her spirit famished. Now their lovemaking was filled with emotion, emotion that gave it meaning. He whispered, "Reva," and kissed her while he loved her, and every thrust of his loins was like a reiteration of her name in movement, glorifying her. Their moment of climax was a true consummation, uniting them wholly in heart, as well as flesh, making them complete, and they called out each other's names in the same moment. Afterward they lay together, enfolded in each other's arms, while their heartbeats slowed to peace and contentment.

At last Reva raised herself on one elbow to look down at him. Her gaze fell on the small bedside lamp, the only light in the room, and she made a slight movement toward it. But he stopped her. "This time let's keep the light on so that I can see you," he said.

"This time?" she asked, teasing him. "When was last time?"

"A strange woman came to my room on the night of the reception," he said, looking at her askance.

"Forward hussy!"

"That's what I thought. I only let her stay because she reminded me of you."

Reva cocked a mischievous eyebrow. "Any good?"

He smiled, and her heart turned over. "Not as good as you." She chuckled and began to kiss his chest. "What about you?" he asked. "Has your life been at all interesting?"

"Oh, yes. There was this really spectacular man a few nights ago."

"Spectacular? Hmm . . ."

"I'm telling you, he was a superstud who knew *every* move."

"Should I be jealous?"

"Definitely."

She met his eyes and saw the humor in their depths. Suddenly it reached his mouth, and he gave a shout of laughter, pulling her close. She began to laugh, too, rejoicing and giving thanks that they'd rediscovered laughter. It had been such a long, lonely time since they'd shared that blessing.

"Come here," he said. *"Come here."*

Joyously she did so, seeking the renewal of the miracle that she'd lost, and had been given back to her. And it was given back again and again.

Reva awoke to find herself lying in Demetrio's arms. The room was filled with golden light. She propped herself up and looked down on his sleeping face, feeling a smile spread throughout her whole body. Last night she'd made love and been made love to with a thoroughness that left her feeling at peace with the entire world. Her lover's face was gentle in sleep, the harsh lines smoothed out, the mouth softened as she had seldom seen it by day. He looked young and vulnerable. She laid her lips tenderly on his and immediately felt his arms go around her.

When they drew apart, his eyes were open. "We didn't dream it, did we?" he asked.

She shook her head. "You were in my room that night," she said. It was a statement, not a question.

He looked cautious. "What will happen if I say yes?"

"Stop negotiating like a businessman, and tell me."

"All right. Yes, I was in your room. I had to be sure you were there. You turned over and touched me, so I told you it was only a dream and got out as soon as I could. I was afraid you'd vanish again if you awoke and found me."

"And the next day you'd gone."

"I had to. I was scared. There were so many misunderstandings between us, I didn't want any more. But it's all right, isn't it?"

"It is now, but—" she hesitated "—is it ever all right between us for more than a short time?"

"It could be. We've found the way. Stay with me, Reva. Stay with me forever. Don't you see that we belong together?"

She sighed. "You make it sound so simple."

"It *is* simple. Think of how we are together. Think of last night... of all the other nights in the past... of all there could be in the future...."

"It was never the nights that were the problem," she reminded him. "They're so perfect that they just confuse me. We can sleep together, but can we live together?"

"We can try. We understand each other better now. We've learned our lessons." He tightened his arms. "Say you'll stay with me."

"Demetrio, please—"

"Say it," he insisted.

But he knew he'd overplayed his hand when he saw the withdrawal in her face. "It's too soon, Demetrio. Please don't press me. I need to think."

He sighed and released her. "I don't see what there is to think about," he said. "It's so obvious—" He checked himself, unwilling to risk damaging their new empathy. "All right, we'll do it your way." He controlled his voice. There came a point in all negotiations when he knew the other side was preparing to concede and all that was left was maneuvering for position. He was adept at hiding his impatience and bringing things to a successful conclusion.

Reva kissed him and got out of bed. He lay back and enjoyed watching her as she moved around the room, naked. Pleasure and satisfaction pervaded him at the thought of having her back with him all the time.

"Aren't you getting up?" she asked.

"I'd rather you came back here."

"It's Sunday," she reminded him. "Last night the count dropped a strong hint that we're all expected at church this morning. From the way he talked, it's the highlight of his week."

"I warned you he was a pillar of the community." Demetrio yawned and got out of bed. "Now I remember. He's donated a stained glass window to the local church, and it's going to be unveiled at this morning's service. He'd be deeply offended if we're not there to admire it."

"And at all costs he mustn't be offended," Reva said, teasing him.

Demetrio gave a wry grin. "Whatever it takes to get Nicoletta walking up the aisle on Guido's arm."

Two hours later they joined the sedate party entering the village church. The count sat impassive as his generosity was praised, and modestly declined an invitation to unveil the window. It was the priest who removed the screen and revealed the stained glass. It was a beautiful work of art, divided into four sections, illustrating the parable of the prodigal son. Finally the priest climbed into the pulpit and delivered a sermon based on the parable, broadened to include the whole subject of reconciliation.

The warm sun streamed in through the windows onto Reva, making her slightly sleepy. The theme seemed a perfect one for her life at this moment. She'd fled, but now it seemed as if she were returning home again and Demetrio's arms were open in welcome. He seemed different. She wasn't sure exactly how. Perhaps that was why she had hesitated before making the final commitment. But there seemed to be a new gentleness and sensitivity about him that gave her hope. Surely now they could find the mutual understanding that would make life together possible....

As they left the church, she said, "I think I'll walk home."

"I'll come with you," Demetrio said at once.

"No." She gave him a smile of reassurance. "I want to be alone. I need some time to think—just a little time."

He returned her smile and gave a little nod. "I'll be waiting."

She strolled back very slowly. Her heart leapt at the thought of returning to Demetrio, but her mind still harbored uneasy thoughts. Chief among them was the memory of a firm called Leddrio Fiscale. They were fi-

nancial specialists who'd given Demetrio a job when he'd
been young and green. They'd cheated him, stolen his
ideas and thrown him out. He'd never forgotten or forgiven.

Reva knew all about it, because during the year she'd
lived with him the firm had gotten into difficulties. The
three men at the top were the same ones who had injured
him, and Reva had been treated to a truly awesome dis-
play of delayed revenge. Demetrio had exerted all his
terrible power to deny them the rescuing financing they
needed. Reva had heard him on the telephone at all
hours, calling in favors and, if that failed, resorting to
outright threats. Finally, when Leddrio was on the ropes,
he'd bought the firm cheap, confronted the three men he
hated and given them five minutes to get out of the
building or be removed by the security guards.

"All these years," she'd said to him. "You never let go
of your grudge?"

And he'd answered, "Revenge is a dish best eaten
cold."

But what had astounded her more than anything was
that he'd sold the firm a week later. After all that effort,
he'd tossed it away almost as soon as he'd gained it. He'd
done what he wanted, and now the financial markets, his
rivals, his opponents, even his friends, knew, if they
hadn't known before, that Demetrio Corelli never slept
until an injury had been avenged. But once the point had
been made, he'd lost interest.

Reva had later learned that the three men who'd lost
out were widely despised, and Demetrio was held to have
done everyone a favor. Furthermore, the innocent members of the firm had had their jobs protected, and Leddrio had been set back on its feet. But it was a friend on
the Milan stock exchange who had told her this. It

wouldn't have occurred to Demetrio to justify his actions, even to his wife.

That memory came back to her now, providing the one tiny cloud over her joy. Might Demetrio want her back only to throw her out and demonstrate that *he* would be the one to end their marriage? It seemed impossible, yet she knew his tendency to conduct his personal and business life by the same principles.

No, she thought passionately. *I won't believe it. This time it's different. He's changed. I know he has.*

The shadows cleared. The night's loving had left her satiated, joyful, and at this moment it seemed as if the whole world belonged to her.

A bright voice broke into her reverie. "Good morning, *signora.*" Looking up, she saw that she'd arrived at the little jetty belonging to the Villa Torvini. Guido was sitting there in a small motorboat. She greeted him and took the hand he held out to help her into the boat. At once he started the engine and headed out onto the lake. Reva threw her head back and let the breeze stream through her hair.

"Shouldn't you be taking Nicoletta out?" she said, laughing.

"I'll be taking her later this afternoon. But I haven't used this boat for a few months, and I was just making sure the engine was running smoothly." He slowed the boat and turned it gently. "How do you like Lake Como?"

"I think it's a beautiful place, a photographer's dream."

"I hope you and Demetrio will often come to stay when Nicoletta and I are married."

"You're quite sure it's going to happen, then?"

He gave a confident, happy smile. "I think so. Papà likes to huff and puff, but he is a good businessman, and in the end he will say yes."

"What has being a good businessman got to do with your marriage?"

"We have a company much like your husband's, only smaller. For some time now, Demetrio and Papà have been circling each other like cats over the linkup. Torvini needs Corelli money, and Corelli needs Torvini distribution depots. The deal will be good for both sides, although perhaps Demetrio needs it more than we do."

"Why do you say that?" Reva asked, in a voice she barely recognized as her own.

"Because if we have to, we can get money elsewhere. But Demetrio *must* have the use of our depots. Building his own would take too much time, and he needs extra space quickly." Guido gave a youthful, guileless laugh. "I'm afraid the position annoys him very much. He's so used to calling the shots, but this time Papà's calling them, and that galls Demetrio, although he hides it very well."

"Yes, he hides things very well," Reva murmured.

Guido looked at her curiously. "You didn't know this?"

"No, I've never taken much int—never interfered with my husband's business affairs," she corrected herself hastily.

"Once it's all gone through, the firms will be tied together pretty firmly. It makes sense to cement the arrangement with a marriage."

"Yes, I can see that," Reva said. Her smiling face gave no hint of her inner turmoil. "Would you mind taking me back now? I'm feeling a little sick."

Guido immediately headed back to shore. He chatted pleasantly as they went, unaware of having shattered Reva. Beneath her pleasant manner Reva was seething. As soon as she was ashore, she hurried up to her room.

Demetrio was there, and he smiled when he saw her. "Come here," he said happily. "Come and kiss me." His smiled faded as he took in her stormy face. "What is it?"

"I should have known, shouldn't I?" she said bitterly. "I should have known better than to think you could ever be anything but a scheming, calculating, hardnosed, business-obsessed monster. But, like a fool, I thought you'd changed. I thought things could be different between us."

He stared. "I don't know what you're talking about."

"Don't you? Then suppose I say 'Torvini distribution depots'? Does that help your memory?"

Demetrio cursed. He'd gone pale. "Who told you that?"

"Guido. Naturally he saw no reason not to. How could he guess that you'd deliberately kept me in the dark so that you could manipulate me more easily?"

"That's not true," he said quickly.

"Of course it's true. You can stop pretending now. Oh, you were so convincing. This was all for Nicoletta's happiness, you said. 'All for the greater good of Corelli Industriale' wouldn't have sounded nearly so touching. You were always brilliant at knowing which button to push. More fool me for being taken in again, when I knew what you were like."

"You don't know. You haven't the least idea," he said harshly. "You always jump to conclusions."

"Did I jump to conclusions this time, Demetrio? Is there no big deal hanging on this wedding?"

He took a deep breath. "It's not quite like that," he said carefully.

"Whatever it's like, the important thing is that you concealed it from me."

"Of course I did. I knew you'd misunderstand, just as you have done. I want this deal, but I want Nicoletta's happiness more."

"They just happen to tie in together rather conveniently."

"It was through business that I got to know Torvini and Nicoletta met Guido. Reva, I beg you, don't make an issue of this."

"You mean don't rock the boat. But which boat, Demetrio?"

He tore his hair. "Why must you always think the worst of me?"

"Experience," she snapped.

"If you'd ever bothered to interest yourself in my work, you'd have learned by now how often business and family go hand in hand. There's nothing dishonest in that."

"You don't call it dishonest to play on my feelings to get me to stay with you?" she demanded furiously.

Demetrio gave a short, mirthless laugh. "You once boasted of having no more feelings where I was concerned. Has that changed?"

She drew a swift breath at what was obviously an attempt to trap her. But if Demetrio thought he could lure her into an admission, he was wrong. "My feelings for you are what they've been for the past year," she said firmly. "Distrust and anger."

"So it was distrust and anger that sent you into my arms last night, was it?" he asked grimly.

"It was madness, and now that I'm sane again I regret it. You'll never act like a dictator with me again."

"I was never a dictator. That was all in your imagination."

"Was it my imagination that you locked me up to stop me defying your 'authority'?"

He threw up his hands. "*Maria Vergine.* That again!"

"Yes, that again. That always. It'll never go away, because it sums up what you are and why I should never trust you. You haven't really changed. Your methods are just more sophisticated. The ties of affection work so much better than bolts and bars, don't they?"

"I never claimed to have changed, Reva. I am what I am. I'm not sentimental, you know that."

"No, you're not sentimental!" she cried scathingly. "You're cruel, cold, hard, and calculating. You'd manipulate your own wife and sister to get a good deal!"

Demetrio stared at her in horror. The beautiful mouth that had moved so sweetly against his was distorted now, pouring out terrible accusations, and as so often before in their quarrels, he felt a dreadful numbing of his brain. The mind that moved like quicksilver in a boardroom brawl could be reduced to tripping over itself when confronted by this woman whom he feared to hurt, and feared to lose, in equal measure.

He cast around frantically for some words that would convey the depths of his pain and fear, but without sacrificing any of his pride. There were none to be found. The best he could manage were "You don't understand how business is done. It isn't…how it looks. If you knew more . . . you'd realize that."

"In other words, run along and mind my own business?" she said furiously.

He'd been trying so hard not to put it like that that he had a strong sense of injustice. Furthermore, they were quarreling in English, the language Reva still reverted to when she was angry. His English was excellent for business purposes, but he couldn't match her swift flow of colorful phrases.

"Very well," he said coldly. "If you want to put it like that, maybe it's best. I can't disentangle family and business just because you get overemotional about something that's actually very simple. I suggest you stick to what you know."

"Overemotional," she echoed, aghast. "You treat me with total contempt—"

"I didn't—"

"You deceive me. You let me discover all over again that you're cynical, arrogant, overbearing, indifferent to my feelings and ready to ride roughshod over any chance of reviving our marriage, and when I dare to protest at your priorities and your twisted morals *I'm* being overemotional? How dare you!"

"As always, you distort everything just to make your argument," he said coldly. "I did . . . I did what was necessary—"

"Necessary for *your* purposes."

"My purposes should be your purposes. We're husband and wife. We should be working for the same thing, but you—" At last his pain burst through into words. *"You have never been a real wife to me."*

She stared at him in shocked silence. When she found her voice, it was thin and utterly unlike hers.

"There's nothing more to say, then," she whispered, and left the room.

Ten

In the profusion of activities at the Villa Torvini, it was possible for two people to avoid each other without attracting much comment. In the next few days, Reva and Demetrio applied themselves assiduously to this task. He took more fishing expeditions, and she began exploring the scenery with her cameras. When they were together in the company of others, they still managed to appear cordial, but it was a strain.

One morning, as they went down to the breakfast room together, Demetrio regarded her casual jeans and sweater with raised eyebrows. "I'm climbing hills," she explained. "I've heard of some interesting rock formations nearby, and I'd like to take pictures."

"Is anyone going with you?"

"No, it's not fair to ask other people to hang around while I'm clicking." She turned to a maid who had just come in. "Is that my packed lunch? Lovely. Thank you."

When the maid had gone, she said pleasantly, "Are you going fishing again?"

"No, I— Reva..."

"Excuse me." She'd noticed the countess trying to attract her attention, and she went over to her, smiling. She didn't see Demetrio again before she left.

She set her feet on a steep path and walked for two hours, then stopped at a trattoria in a tiny village. She drank a glass of wine at an outside table looking down at the lake, which now seemed a long way below.

"Do you mind if I take this seat?"

Looking up, she saw a plump, middle-aged man with a friendly face, wearing a uniform. She smiled to indicate her compliance, and he seated himself on the bench beside her. They fell easily into conversation. He introduced himself as Tonio, the local police chief.

"You surely can't get much crime in this peaceful little place?" Reva said.

"True," he said, a hint of regret in his voice. "My men and I do more rescuing than arresting. About a mile beyond here, it becomes dangerous. The side of the hill veers in, making a straight drop, and the path becomes narrow. Be careful if you're taking pictures. Don't get so absorbed that you step backward over the edge."

Reva promised and, after chatting for a little while longer, rose to go. Tonio walked part of the way with her, and they separated at the little police station.

Walking briskly, she soon came to the place he'd mentioned, and understood why he'd warned her. The path not only was narrow and steep, but also began to wind sharply, so it was impossible to see more than a few yards ahead at a time. Several times she found herself suddenly staring down at a hair-raising drop. Fascinated, she lay down on her stomach, clicking her shutter madly, eager to explore every facet of such dramatic beauty.

Still lying down, she put in another roll of film, then got carefully to her feet. The day was turning out better than she'd hoped. But as soon as she rounded the next corner, she had a shock. A man was standing there, leaning against the rock, looking back in her direction, almost as if he were waiting for her. He had a cold, hawklike face, and a frisson went through her as she realized where she had seen him before. He'd been driving the car that had followed her just before she left Milan.

For a moment they watched each other. Then Reva walked defiantly toward him, raising the camera until it was level with his face. She clicked the shutter, lowered the camera and said calmly, "I didn't get one the first time."

For a moment, the man was quite still. Then his arm shot out so fast that she didn't see it. He seized the strap and twisted it about her neck, choking her. Holding her with one hand, he wrenched the camera free and tossed it down the mountain. "And nobody will ever see that one," he said with deadly softness. "You're very foolish, *signora*. You interfere in things that are none of your business. Heed this warning, for it's the only one you'll get. The next time—"

He broke off and jerked her forward so that she had a terrifying vision of the endless depths. "The next time—" he repeated.

It had happened so fast that Reva barely had time to react. Now she found her heart thumping with horror, less at the danger than at her own helplessness. She couldn't even cry out, because the leather strap cut off her voice. It was pressing into her neck. She couldn't breathe. She was beginning to black out....

Suddenly she found herself free. The strap was loose, and she could breathe again. She stood heaving in great lungfuls of air while her brain seemed to crash against her skull and the mountains spun wildly around her. Then, as sense returned, she realized that there were sounds coming from behind her, and she turned to see her attacker thrust back against the granite wall, with Demetrio's hands about his throat. She was still too sick and dizzy to do anything but stagger back against the wall and cling to it. From this angle, she could see Demetrio's eyes, full of murderous hate as he confronted the man who had tried to harm her. A new dread rose in her. For his own sake, Demetrio mustn't kill this man.

"Demetrio...no..." The words came out as a whispered croak, but he heard them and glanced at her. It was the briefest look, but it was his undoing. His opponent seized the moment, thundering a punch into his stomach and then kicking him violently. Demetrio went staggering back, gasping violently for air. Reva screamed when she saw his foot slip, and she launched herself forward, grasping for his hand. The next moment she was standing at the edge, her hands empty, crying Demetrio's name as he went over the edge and down into the gorge.

Without waiting to see what had happened, the man took to his heels. Reva flung herself to the ground, trying to see Demetrio through her tears. "Oh, God," she sobbed. "No...please...no..."

She heard her own name carried on the wind, and for a moment she thought she was going mad. Then she realized that Demetrio was calling to her. Inching forward on her stomach, she saw him far below, clinging to a ledge, his arms stretched out at full-length. The realization that she was all that stood between him and death cleared her brain. "I'm going for help," she yelled. "Hold on."

She struggled to her feet and tore back in the direction of the village, bursting in on Toni, who had been deep in his afternoon snooze. In a moment he was on the telephone, calling in the local reserves, for these were mountain people, always primed for this situation. "My car's outside," he said tersely. "Show me exactly where your husband is."

On the way he demanded a description of her attacker. Reva told as much as she could recall, and he started putting details out on his radio. "My men will pick him up," he assured her.

She barely heard him. She had closed her eyes and was praying as she had never prayed in her life. "Let him still be there.... Let him be alive... *Please, let him be alive....*"

When they reached the spot, she hardly dared look, but when she did peer over Demetrio was still there, still holding on, but his face was turned sideways, as if he'd lost consciousness and was gripping the ledge by blind instinct.

Three young men had driven up behind them in a heavy car, from which they now descended, armed with ropes that they attached to the car. Two of them took up position holding on to the ropes, while the third calmly shinned down the rock face to Demetrio. Reva lay on her stomach on the edge, staring down into the abyss, hardly daring to watch, yet unable to tear her gaze away.

At last the climber reached Demetrio and began securing him with ropes. Then came the slow, careful haul upward, with the two young men at the top drawing the rope in. Inch by inch they rose. Reva could see now that Demetrio was moving a little, using his hands to brace himself against the rock. "Thank God!" she whispered. "Oh, thank God!"

At last they reached the top, and Demetrio lay sprawled on the grass, his eyes closed. Reva knelt beside him as they opened, and smiled shakily at him, hoping to see a smile back. But he only stared at her vaguely, and he didn't respond until the sergeant said, "Now we'll take you to the hospital, *signore.*"

That roused him enough to say, "No hospital. Nothing's broken. Just take me home."

They demurred, but he insisted, and at last Tonio agreed to take him directly to the Villa Torvini. Reva paused to thank the three young men, then got into the back of the car with him. He looked at her. "Are you all right?" he muttered.

She nodded, and he closed his eyes. Reva leaned forward to speak to the sergeant. "Could you please use your radio to call a doctor to the villa?" she asked.

He nodded and did so. Demetrio didn't open his eyes until they arrived, and then he insisted on getting out and walking up the long flights of steps unaided. "Please don't be stupid," Reva begged. "Let them carry you."

"That would be showing weakness," he growled, "and I can't afford to do that."

"Why on earth not?"

"Because Torvini is a business rival, and you said yourself, I never let anything get in the way of business."

He relented so far as to allow Guido to offer him an arm, but when Nicoletta fluttered around him, all concern, he summoned up a reassuring smile. "Don't be silly, I'm fine," he said, with a fair impersonation of cheerfulness. "Take care of Reva."

He made it to the top on his own feet, but then he swayed, his eyes closing again. Count Torvini barked out some orders, and some male servants carried Demetrio upstairs. The doctor appeared almost immediately, and after a thorough examination he announced that Demetrio was suffering from nothing worse than bruises and shock. Reva went downstairs with the news, and found Count Torvini hearing the story from Tonio. He pronounced himself inexpressibly shocked.

"That such a thing should have happened to my guest fills me with shame," he declared to Reva.

"Please don't feel like that," she begged. "I really—" She stopped suddenly. She'd been about to explain why she'd been attacked, but now she recalled that the count already disapproved of her work. The full details would only earn his further disapproval, and Nicoletta would suffer. "I really feel all right now," she amended hastily. "I think I'll go up to Demetrio."

"Would you like to have dinner served up there tonight?" the countess asked kindly.

"Yes, please."

The doctor was just leaving the bedroom. "All he needs is rest, but as he seems disinclined to take it, I've given him something that will make him sleep," he explained.

"Thank you," Reva said gratefully.

"He'll be very stiff and sore tomorrow, but nothing lasting."

Reva slipped into the bedroom. The shutters had been drawn halfway, and outside the light was fading fast. In the dim light she could see Demetrio only as a lump in the bed, turned away from her, his shoulders hunched. From the way he was breathing, it was clear that he was very deeply asleep.

Reva stripped and showered. She was aching in every limb from tension. When her supper was served, she found it almost impossible to eat, and at last she left the food and went out onto the balcony. It was in the last moments before twilight turned to night. Down by the lake she could see lights twinkling in the villages, and far off the snow-capped mountains loomed silently.

The cool air was balm to her fevered spirit. What had happened today had thrown her into turmoil. For one dreadful hour, everything in her life had been concentrated into one overwhelming question: Would Demetrio live or die? And she'd known then that if he died, life would hold nothing else for her. She loved him. If she'd had any lingering doubts left, this had dispelled them. He might be the most awkward, difficult, maddening and infuriating man alive, but she loved him.

She went over to the bed and sat on it. He was sunk in a deep sleep, lying on his back, his hair tousled and his mouth gentler than she ever saw it when he was awake. Very gently she leaned forward and touched his lips with her own.

"I love you," she whispered. "And somehow, from now on, we're going to have to make a go of it, because I can't do without you. I found that out today."

She watched over him with a kind of yearning possessiveness. He was hers. She'd nearly lost him, but now she had him safe, and she would keep him safe. All her normal sophistication seemed to have been peeled away, revealing only raw instinct beneath, and her instinct was to protect him at all costs. He was her treasure, and if it had been possible, she would have locked her treasure away where the world couldn't get at it. She managed to laugh at her own thoughts. But then the laugh died as illumination came to her.

Demetrio had once locked her up to stop her going into danger. She'd railed at him, furiously insisting that his action sprang from selfishness, not love. But now the same fierce protectiveness had come alive in her, and she saw that it really was love—not modern love, not the civilized love of give-and-take, of polite manners, of pride and sophistication. This was basic and elemental, and it grew out of need. If the feelings that had turned him into her jailer were anything like the ones that swept her at this moment, then he loved her with a completeness that was thrilling. That didn't justify his action, but it enabled her to see it in perspective, without the distorting mirror of resentment.

But she saw other things, too, things that troubled her deeply. She saw that her regimented childhood had caused her to make a religion of her personal freedom, and that because of it she'd given too little attention to Demetrio's feelings and needs. She'd thought she could marry and go on in the old way, so she'd dismissed his protests as a selfish desire to fetter her.

Selfish. She tried out the word and discovered that it fitted her much better than her husband. He'd married her because he wanted to be with her, and all he'd asked was that she consider his suffering before endangering herself. But she'd never credited him with suffering, because until this afternoon she hadn't understood what suffering was.

"But I know now," she whispered to him. "I've been selfish and thoughtless, and I left it so late before I even tried to understand you. But I've grown up now. I love you. Do you hear? I love you. I'll spend my life making it up to you. When you wake up, we're going to have lots to talk about. But until then, sleep, my darling, while I watch over you and keep you safe."

She opened her eyes several hours later to find that it was dawn. Demetrio hadn't moved. She stood up, stretched, and went to splash some cold water on her face. When she came back, he'd opened his eyes. She went to him, smiling. "You look better," she said happily.

He frowned. He still seemed to be groggy. "What happened?" he asked.

"You found a man attacking me and pulled him off me," she said. "Don't you remember?"

"Yes," he said, rubbing his eyes. "It's coming back. I heard him say something . . . something about you interfering. Or did I imagine that?"

"No."

"What did he mean?"

"Never mind that now. I want to tell you—"

"I would like to know what he meant, Reva."

She sighed. "He was trying to frighten me off a story I'm working on."

She had the feeling that the sleep had left his brain abruptly. "What?" he said.

"I've been taking some pictures that certain people would like stopped."

He looked at her with grim humor. His eyes had grown hard. "Of course. When aren't you? I had hoped you could leave work behind while we were here, but it seems not."

"I did leave work behind," she protested. "This is about a story I did in Milan. He followed me here. He tried to run me off the road just before we left. I thought I'd imagined it, but it was the same man."

"Well, that makes everything lovely for you, doesn't it?"

"*What?*"

"That's how you like it best, the excitement, the danger. You can't live without it, can you? So much more thrilling than dreary domesticity with a man you neither like nor trust. I'm sorry I butted in and spoiled your fun."

"Demetrio, please don't talk like that. I've been longing for you to awake so that I can tell you how I feel."

"I think you've already told me that, very thoroughly."

"No...wait...things are different..." she said wildly. Her dismay was growing as she realized how hard it would be to open her heart to this grimly ironic man.

But Demetrio's expression didn't soften. "Come, Reva, surely you're not going to get dewy-eyed because I came galloping to the rescue? I'm sure you could have dealt with him very efficiently without me."

"Well, I couldn't," she said stormily. "It was a mercy you turned up just then—"

"Surely not! You said he was only trying to scare you!"

"He was succeeding very thoroughly. Can't you be quiet while I say I'm grateful?"

"All right. Consider it said." Demetrio sounded bored.

She stared at him, sick with disappointment and disillusion. "You won't give an inch, will you?" she asked, dazed.

"Just following your excellent example, dear wife. *You* never give an inch. I've decided you were right all the time."

She made one last, despairing effort. "Demetrio, why were you up there just then, so close behind me?"

"Pure accident. If you're daring to suggest that I was trailing after you, hoping for a reconciliation, you can forget it. Nothing would have persuaded me."

"It never occurred to me," she said coldly. She was too hurt to think clearly, or to detect the faint note of over-emphasis in Demetrio's voice.

She rose from the bed. "I haven't told the Torvinis what really happened," she said. "They think it was a stray thug. The truth wouldn't make them think more kindly of us. Count Torvini already disapproves of me for having a career. Just like you."

"I never disapproved of your career, Reva. It was just its all-consuming nature that hur—that troubled me. I felt I was fitted into the spare moments when you had nothing better to do."

"That's not true." Then she added hastily, "But I can see how it may have looked like that. Demetrio, please let me explain—"

"Is that really necessary? We'll just be going back over old ground, and it just leads to quarrels."

"We didn't quarrel in the beginning," she said, with a touch of wistfulness in her tone that she couldn't banish.

"Because we could always distract ourselves another way. But that was a mistake, wasn't it, Reva? Because without it we'd have seen the truth much sooner."

"The truth?"

"That we don't belong together, and never have. I've heard you say so yourself."

"Yes," she said after a moment. "Yes, I have, haven't I? But that was a long time ago—"

"It was just a few days ago. I realize that our conversations don't come high on your list of priorities, but you usually manage better than that."

"It may have been only a few days ago in time, but it seems like much longer. If you'd only let me explain what I've been thinking..."

His eyes were mocking. "You surely haven't allowed yourself to get sentimental over a trivial incident? Come, my dear, you're usually above such weakness."

The words hit her like a blow to the stomach. Sentimentality and weakness—the two things that Demetrio despised above all. She'd been deluding herself. She managed to shrug and speak lightly. "I've no more time for weakness than you have yourself. In that, at least, we're well matched. Unfortunately, it's not enough."

"How nice to find something we agree on," he said ironically, and she turned away to hide the despair on her face.

Demetrio lay back on his pillow, weary from the effort to appear nonchalant, and relieved that she'd looked away before she could discern his true feelings in his eyes. He wanted to curse when he remembered how he'd hurried after her up the mountain, hoping for a chance to talk and perhaps make things right, how naively he'd delighted in coming to her aid, how glad he'd been to discover that she still needed him for something.

And it had all turned out to be a sick joke. The whole thing was nothing but an episode in her private adventure. To Reva such moments were proof that she was a success. He felt like Saint George, galloping off to rescue the maiden from the dragon—only to discover that she was armed with a flamethrower.

Well, no more, he promised himself. She'd made a fool of him for the last time. He'd grit his teeth and play this farce out for just as long as it took to get his sister married, and then he need never see his wife again.

Eleven

As soon as possible, Reva slipped into the village and called Benno's number, but all she got was his answering machine. She identified herself as Alicia, related what had happened, and begged him to take care of himself. She tried calling again the next day and the day after, but there was still only the answering machine.

After the third call, she returned to the villa to find an atmosphere of violent tension. She was just in time to see Guido fling himself into his boat and roar away, and when she climbed the stairs she found Nicoletta looking out over the lake with tears in her eyes. "What's wrong?" Reva asked quickly. "Have you and Guido quarreled?"

"Oh no, never," Nicoletta said quickly. She gave a wobbly smile that touched Reva's heart. "He's asked his father for his consent to our marriage...."

"And the count has refused? I can't believe it."

Nicoletta shook her head. "He agrees," she said, but her tone was still doleful.

"Then what is there to cry about?" Reva asked.

"He wants a long engagement—at least a year."

"I see," Reva said grimly. "So that's his game. He hopes Guido will tire of you."

"No," Nicoletta protested. "Our engagement is to be announced at once."

Reva suppressed the thought that this was just a clever ploy. The count would go through an elaborate pantomime of consent and sign his agreement with Demetrio, and in a year the engagement would be broken. She wouldn't hurt Nicoletta by expressing this opinion, but it was blindingly clear to her.

She hurried into the house and found Demetrio. "Are you going to let him get away with this?" she demanded.

"Just tell me how you think it can be avoided," he retorted. "Torvini gives his consent, very publicly. What am I to do? Accuse him of bad faith? Would that improve the outlook for Nicoletta? The best I can do is to play a waiting game—put clauses into the deal that will give me some leverage over him in a year's time. But you're always the same. For you there must be impulsive action."

"A waiting game is no use to us," she reminded him.

"If you want fast action, you're talking to the wrong person," Demetrio snapped. "Guido's the only one who can do anything. Let him be a man and stand up to his father. If he can't do that, perhaps Nicoletta's better off without him."

"Don't say that to her. She's unhappy enough as it is."

"It's true, and you know it. Would *you* want to marry such a milksop?"

She shrugged. "My taste in men is appalling. I don't trust myself anymore."

His mouth twisted into a cynical smile. "Very wise."

Whatever game Count Torvini was playing, he was working fast. The grand engagement dinner party was set for two days ahead, and despite the short notice, most of the aristocratic families staying along the shore accepted. Reva prepared for the evening with deep foreboding. The count's surprise decision had presented her with a dilemma. There was no way she could stay with Demetrio indefinitely until the wedding had taken place, but she didn't want to blight Nicoletta's prospects.

She was to remember the evening of the dinner party all her life.

From the first moment, there was an air of tension. The countess announced that three guests had canceled at the very last moment. The first couple to arrive seemed ill at ease and looked oddly at their host. They were followed by others who acted in the same way. Then the countess was called to the telephone and came back with a strained smile to announce further cancellations.

Nicoletta was in despair. "They disapprove of me," she said.

"Nonsense," Reva said at once. "If that were true, they wouldn't have accepted in the first place."

"They accepted because they didn't know why they'd been invited," Nicoletta insisted. "But now they've heard rumors about the engagement and they're showing how they feel."

Reva tried to reassure her, but there was a concertedness about the actions that made her uneasy, too.

At last it was clear that nobody else was coming, and about half the original party sat down to dinner. It was an uncomfortable meal. Some of those present didn't know what had gone wrong, and the ones who did were too embarrassed to talk. Then a servant came to call the count to the telephone. He took the call in a room next door, and a few moments later the guests heard him shouting, "Lies ... lies ... I will sue...."

Guido rose hastily and went to his father. After a moment, the countess followed him. An almost visible frisson ran through the guests. "Someone has told him," said a man three seats down from Reva.

"Told him what?" Reva asked. "What on earth is going on?"

"*Time & Tide* came out this afternoon," said another man. "There's an article in it about slum properties. Appalling places. The pictures were unbelievable. Children with rat bites, that sort of thing. The writer reckons he's traced the line of ownership back to Torvini. He can call it lies if he likes, but the writer had gone to a lot of trouble to check his facts. It sounded true enough to me."

"Surely that's impossible," a woman said. "He's such a splendid, upright man. Nobody has done more to protect public morals."

"Public and private morals aren't always the same thing," someone said, and there was general laughter.

"It sounds very convincing," the first man said. With a quick glance over his shoulder, he pulled some sheets of paper out of his inner pocket, and spread them out on the table. "I tore these out just before we came."

A little crowd formed around him. Reva didn't join it. She was staring straight ahead while cold horror crept through her body. Demetrio was looking at her in silence.

It was Paulo Alessi who spoke next. "I know that company. It's little more than a front for another one called Royale, and I know for a fact that Torvini has a controlling interest in Royale.''

People began to look at each other. "It's true, then?" they asked, aghast.

"It's true," Alessi said. "Look, most of us have business interests, and none of us are saints. But there are limits. I'd be ashamed to house pigs like this, let alone humans."

There was a murmur of agreement from the men and women. As Alessi had said, they weren't saints, but they were decent people, and this sickened them.

Suddenly a silence fell. Heads turned in the direction of the door. Count Torvini stood there, his face pale. "It's lies," he choked out. "How can you believe the filth that appears in that rag?"

"But you do have a controlling interest in Royale?" Alessi challenged him.

Torvini did not reply. It was another voice that said, "Yes, we do."

Torvini turned on his son, who had come into the room behind him and now stood there with a face like death. *"You,"* he said scathingly. *"You will be silent."*

Guido didn't reply. He walked past his father to where the group was standing with the article. "May I?" he asked politely, and lifted the sheets of paper. He read for a moment, then turned to look silently at his father. To the watchers his face seemed expressionless, but Torvini must have seen something there, because he screamed, "You are no son of mine if you believe these lies!"

Guido was very still. "Perhaps I had better not be a son of yours if this is what it means," he said. "You've always kept me away from the real decision-making, but I know enough of your arrangements to recognize that these are your companies." A shudder seemed to go through him. "I'm ashamed to be your son."

Torvini lost all control. "How dare you speak to me like that!" he screamed. "You ally yourself with traitors against me. *You—*" He turned his attention to Demetrio, who had been watching the scene coolly. "This is a trick of yours to discredit me. You planned this, you and your wife. Do you think I didn't know who 'Alicia' was?"

"Then you knew more than I did until now," Demetrio told him. "And I suggest, for the sake of your dignity, that we postpone the rest of this discussion for a more suitable time."

"There will never be a better time to tell you that no son of mine will marry into your family," Torvini snapped.

"Marry into *my—?*" Sheer outrage seemed to strike Demetrio dumb. He recovered himself and made a contemptuous gesture toward the article, which lay on the table, clearly displaying the picture of a rat-bitten child. "Do you imagine I would allow such a marriage, that I would permit my sister to connect herself with *this?*"

Guido stepped between them. "That's enough," he said. "I've waited too long to be my own man, but it's not too late." He went to stand in front of Nicoletta, who had risen, her eyes fixed on him. "Nicoletta Corelli," he said quietly, "will you marry a poor man from a disgraced family, a man without a job, without a home, with only his love to offer you?"

Nicoletta smiled at him through her tears. "I want only to be your wife," she said. "Now there is nothing to come between us."

This was how it should be, Reva thought as she watched the young people in each other's arms—heartfelt, simple, with everything else stripped away, and only love left. This was how it had never been for Demetrio and her.

She looked at her husband, but he, too, had his eyes fixed on the young couple. He said nothing.

The party began to break up in embarrassment. Guests muttered perfunctory words and slipped away. Demetrio seemed to come out of a trance. "I think we'd better leave immediately," he said to Reva.

"I, too, am leaving," Guido announced.

"No," Torvini said sharply.

"I must, Papà," Guido said in a gentler voice. "I can't work for you anymore. I must find my own feet. Both you and my mother are invited to my wedding, which will be as soon as possible. After that, we'll see each other when you've put right those properties, and any others like them. Not until then."

"I forbid this," Torvini said hoarsely. "I forbid this wedding."

Guido gave him a pitying look, then drew Nicoletta away, saying, "We have a lot to talk about."

Reva had already started packing when Demetrio came into the room. She looked up and found his eyes on her. They were deadly cold. "It takes my breath away to think that you accused me of deception!" he said. "You're a cool character. I have to give you that."

"Don't talk like that," she cried. "You can't believe that I knew about this. You know I'm not capable of such meanness."

"I thought we'd agreed that neither of us knew the other well. At this moment I'd be glad to know what to believe you capable of."

"Not this," she said passionately. *"Not this."*

He shrugged. "Why not? It's a great story, and your pictures are magnificent. I congratulate you. The sensation you caused tonight must have exceeded your wildest dreams. There will be even more of a sensation in Milan." He glanced sardonically at her luggage. "You're right to get back early. There will be rich fruits from this, and you must be there to pluck them."

"Do you really think I could be so cynical?" she cried out in anguish.

"Not cynical, just professional. You've worked hard for your moment of glory. It nearly cost you your life. You should enjoy it."

"For God's sake, don't talk like that!"

"Like what?"

"As though there were nothing in you but ice."

"But there isn't. You took the rest long ago. Ice suits me very nicely. It appears to suit you, too. Only an ice-cold brain could have pulled this off, living with your prey, day by day, fooling everyone, even me. *Especially* me. Are you proud of yourself for that? But it can't have been difficult, can it? I'm so easily fooled where you're concerned, so eager to believe any good of you, so reluctant to see the bad until it's thrust under my nose. Oh, you did a beautiful job on me, Reva. You even—" He stopped. Something seemed to be choking him. Abruptly he turned his back on her and went to stare out the window at the cold mountains.

Reva felt as if she were sinking into a quagmire. This couldn't be happening. It was a nightmare. But she couldn't awaken from it. She could only fight her way out with all the persuasiveness at her command. Once, perhaps, she might have called on his love to speak for her. But it seemed there was no love left. "Demetrio, listen to me," she pleaded.

"I'm listening." He spoke over his shoulder without looking at her.

"I *am* Alicia. I took those pictures, but I had no idea Torvini owned the apartments. Nobody knew. That was the whole point. He covered his tracks so well. All this time the journalist has been working to unravel the tangle of companies to discover the real owner. I turned in my pictures before we came here, and left him to get on with it."

Demetrio gave a harsh, mirthless laugh. "Do you expect me to believe that you didn't know that he'd found the information and it was about to be published?"

"I *didn't* know. After what happened on the mountain, I tried to call him, but he'd apparently gone into hiding. I've had no contact with him. That's the truth." When he didn't answer, she went to him and forced him to turn around and face her. She nearly wept at the sight of his face. Every vestige of human emotion had been stripped from it. He looked as if he'd died and gone to hell.

"Don't look at me like that," she begged.

"I'd rather not look at you at all." He tried to turn away, but she held on to him. "We can't leave it like this," she begged. "Demetrio, please, you must believe me."

Reluctantly he looked down at her. "Your face is so candid," he said, as if talking to himself, "so innocent and open. You look as if you couldn't conceal a secret or think a harmful thought. And all the time—"

"All the time—what? You can't really believe I've been scheming behind your back. And Nicoletta? What about her? Do you think I'd break her heart?"

"But you haven't broken it. She's triumphed. Torvini's finished. Guido can defy him. They don't need anyone's permission to marry now. Which means you can drop the pretense that I mean anything to you and get away from me quickly.''

''It's not a pretense,'' she said, very pale. ''I love you. I knew that when you nearly died.''

''Please, Reva, there's no need for this. You've won. My congratulations. I no longer have any hold over you, do I? And that must please you more than anything. Now, why don't you finish packing? I still have something to do.''

He wrenched himself free from her grasp and strode from the room. Reva stood frozen, listening to his footsteps echoing on the marble stairs. She could hardly believe the calamity that had come upon her. In the past she'd seen Demetrio angry and bitter, but never before had he turned on her the face of icy rejection she'd seen tonight. By a terrible irony, it had come now, when she had only just discovered the depth of her feelings for him. And it had come too late.

Torvini scowled when he saw Demetrio coming into his office. ''My family and I are leaving,'' Demetrio said. ''You and I have nothing further to say to each other, either privately or in business.''

''You take a high-and-mighty attitude,'' Torvini said, scoffing, ''but you still need my depots. You'll have to come back to me, and when you do, I'll make you pay for this.''

''Nothing in this world could make me have any further connection with you,'' Demetrio said flatly. ''If I could stop my sister taking the name Torvini, I would, but I can't, so I'll have to put up with it. But beyond that, you don't exist as far as I'm concerned. Exploiting your wretched tenants was bad enough, but you did something else, something far worse, for which I'll never forgive you. I used to think revenge was a dish best eaten cold, but *this* revenge I'm going to have now."

His fist shot out in a lightning movement that caught Torvini off guard. The count went reeling back against the wall, and he uttered a high-pitched scream of fear when he saw Demetrio coming after him. But Demetrio didn't strike him again. Instead, he seized his lapels and shook him like a rat. He shook him until Torvini was trembling with shock, and then he threw him down onto a sofa, where he landed sprawling.

"You set your thugs onto my wife," Demetrio said with soft menace. "And you're lucky I don't kill you for that."

He made a gesture as if cleaning some contaminant off his hands, and then he walked out without a backward glance.

Twelve

The day after their return to Milan, Nicoletta and Guido went to the town hall together, and returned with the news that the wedding was set for two weeks hence—the earliest the law allowed. Guido then disappeared for a couple of days. When he came back, he announced that he had a job.

"*I'd* have given you a job," Demetrio said at once.

"I know, and I'm grateful," Guido assured him. "But I want one that I got for myself, on merit, not because of my family."

"Which firm are you going to work for?"

Guido took a deep breath. "I'm going to teach mathematics at a school in Rome."

"What?" Demetrio leapt to his feet. "Do you know what a teacher earns?"

"I'm sure it will seem very little to you," Guido said with his sweet smile, "but it's honest money."

"And we'll be together," Nicoletta said, taking his hand. "That's all that matters."

Demetrio stared at her. "And you seriously think I'll allow you to—?" But then he checked himself, and Reva saw a great weariness settle over him. "Well, if you've made up your mind," he said heavily. "But Rome is so far away."

"It's better like this," Guido said.

"Yes, yes, I suppose so...." Demetrio seemed stunned. When the two young people had gone, he gave Reva a wan smile. "I've learned some wisdom, you see."

"Yes. Trying to keep people by force doesn't work."

"I suppose you'll be leaving now?"

"I'll stay for the wedding, so as not to hurt Nicoletta."

He gave a mirthless laugh. "If you imagine that either of those two notice what anyone else does, you delude yourself. They're in their own world."

"I know. I hope they can make that world last forever."

"Do you think they can?"

"Perhaps. They're wiser than we ever were."

He sighed. "That's true."

In the next two weeks, Demetrio was fully occupied with work. Reva barely saw him. Once, when he returned late, looking worn out, Reva ventured to suggest that he needed more rest.

"I can't rest just now," he said abruptly. "I have a great deal to do at work."

"Because you've lost the Torvini distribution depots?" she asked. "Can you find others?"

"Ah...it doesn't matter," he said—uneasily, it seemed to her. "I don't need them anymore."

"But—"

"It's too complicated to explain," he said brusquely.

"Demetrio, I didn't mean to harm you."

"On the contrary. You did me a favor in revealing the truth about Torvini before I tied my firm to his. I'd have hated to be connected with such a scandal. I'm obliged to you."

But, though his mouth spoke thanks, his eyes were distant, and Reva knew there was no real communication between them.

There was plenty to fill her time, starting with a celebratory lunch with Benno Andrese, who had come out of hiding and was jubilant at their success. As he poured the champagne, he said, "If only you were staying. What achievements we could create together!"

"I can't stay," she said regretfully. "There's nothing for me here anymore."

"But there's everything for you here," he protested. "I've got a string of hot tips to follow up."

Reva shook her head. "There's nothing for me here," she repeated.

She went shopping with Nicoletta for a simple wedding dress. The ceremony was set to take place in a small village church on Demetrio's land. When it was over, the bride and groom would fly away for a short honeymoon in Naples before going straight to Rome, where Nicoletta, too, intended to find a job.

A couple of days before the wedding, Reva set out to explore the whole estate. It was a beautiful place, and anything was better than staying indoors, reflecting on the loneliness that faced her. When it was time to go home, she turned back in the direction of the house, but after only a few yards she stopped. She stayed quite still for a while, fighting an inner battle. Then, as if of their own volition, her feet turned and began to trace a particular path.

Ever since the day they'd left for Lake Como and Demetrio had avoided showing her his childhood home, she'd known that one day she would come here. There seemed little reason for her to bother, now that she was so close to putting her husband out of her life forever, but something drove her on just the same.

She found the little cluster of cottages, all falling down except one, which had been kept in perfect repair. Most curious of all was a small generator that stood outside. The shutters were closed, and the front and back doors locked, but Reva had been taught how to pick a lock by a reformed burglar she'd once photographed, and what she found here presented no problems. In a few minutes, she was inside the tiny cottage.

When her eyes got used to the gloom, she made her way across to the windows and opened the shutters. The late-afternoon sun showed her a room with a stone floor, a wide fireplace, two wooden chairs and a table. Reva looked at them, trying to imagine Demetrio here as a child, for it was clear that nothing had been changed. The table even bore carvings that looked as if they might have been made by a child using a penknife.

The walls were white, and bore a couple of pictures that Mamma Corelli seemed to have cut from magazines, and a decorative plate with a crack in it.

She came to a framed photograph that seemed out of place in the room. The frame was oval, decorated with a slightly raised pattern, and it appeared to be made of gold. That meant that Demetrio himself had put it there, and the middle-aged woman in the picture must be his mother. Reva studied her, seeing the resemblance in the grim, slightly harsh features of a woman whose life had been hard. She might have been any age from forty to sixty.

Beneath the photograph there were words, written directly on the wall, in a hand that Reva recognized as Demetrio's: In this house lived and died Maria Corelli, a poor woman, who had nothing but the love of her son and daughter.

Reva read the notice several times, trying to understand why the simple, dignified words made her want to cry. There was something touching in the way Demetrio had included Nicoletta, who had been only a few weeks old when Maria died. Reva remembered Nicoletta saying how her brother had often spoken to her of their mother, trying to recreate the bond that had been cruelly broken so soon. Here was another clue to his heart, the heart that she had never understood.

Suddenly she remembered him saying, "I wanted to find my eternal home in your arms." He was lonely. He'd been lonely ever since his mother's death, and perhaps even longer. Where Reva had wanted the unpredictability of love, he'd sought the security of love. He'd wanted a true home, and she'd never given him one. She'd thought it was enough to be a passionate lover. It was so easy to understand, now that it was too late.

A flight of stairs led straight up from the main room to the floor above. She went upstairs, wondering if she could identify the room where he'd slept as a boy. She found a main bedroom, probably Maria's, and another, smaller room. She pushed the door open and halted, amazed at what she found.

The little room was almost empty. In one corner was a chest of drawers. In the other, incongruous in the shabby surroundings, was a large television set with a videocassette recorder underneath. There was no antenna attached to the television. It seemed to be there only for use with the VCR, yet there was no sign of any tapes. Puzzled, she turned both machines on. A small light winked, signifying that there was a tape in the recorder. Reva hesitated a moment before her curiosity got the better of her, and she pressed the play button. The machine whirred, and the next moment her own face was on the screen.

Astounded, she sank into the chair and watched intently. After a few seconds, she recognized the tape as a television broadcast she'd done about six months before. But surely, she thought, it had never been shown in Italy. Then she realized that the commentary was in English and there were no Italian subtitles, which meant it had been taped in England. Demetrio must have made special arrangements to have this sent to him.

Impulsively she got up, went over to the chest of drawers and began pulling them open. She found another tape containing a small broadcast she'd done on local television in her hometown. It was five minutes from a hick town in the back of beyond, but Demetrio had tracked it down and had it sent to him.

In another drawer she found copies of newspapers and magazines containing her work, and twelve issues of a monthly photographic magazine for which she wrote a column, that bore her picture. Beneath the last one Reva found the answer. It was a letter from a clipping service, addressed to Demetrio, asking him if he wished to continue receiving all material "concerning or related to Ms. Reva Horden."

She sat down, astounded at the discovery. On this evidence, Demetrio Corelli, the man who proudly boasted that he was unsentimental, stood convicted of the most blatant sentimentality. And this was the place he hadn't wanted her to see.

There was a sound from the doorway, and she turned to find Nicoletta standing there. "I wondered if you'd ever find this," she said. "I hoped so. This room can tell you so much more than my brother can say in words."

"You knew about this? You knew it was why he wouldn't let me come here the day we left for Lake Como?" Nicoletta nodded. "But why didn't you tell me?"

"Because he forbade me to, because his pride won't let him tell you how much he craves for you to stay with him. He talks about the 'aristocratic' Torvini pride, but his own is so much more terrible and inflexible, and he never sees it. He can speak of his love, but not his need. To him, need is a weakness."

"But he told you," Reva said.

"No, I found out by accident. He locked this room and told me it was because the floor wasn't safe. But one day I came here and heard a noise from above. I crept up the stairs and in here without him seeing me. He was watching the tape of you. When it finished, he ran it back to the beginning and watched it again—and then again. When he discovered me there, he was furious and ordered me out. We never spoke of it, but I know he comes here and shuts himself in this room for hours. Reva, look around you and see the truth. There is so much love here."

"Yes," Reva said slowly. "There is love here. But then why—?"

"Because he is the way he is," Nicoletta said wisely. "Just as you are the way you are. Neither of you can change, but you can love each other despite your differences. When you tell him you've been here—"

"No," Reva said at once. "I can't tell him, and neither must you. If he wants me to know, he'll tell me."

"But it's so simple...."

"It isn't simple at all. Some things can't be forced. I guess pride is one of them."

"And love is another," Nicoletta said. "But if you have love, you don't need pride."

"Then perhaps we never had love. Demetrio and I misunderstood each other all along the way. Maybe we were never meant to do anything else."

"I don't believe that," Nicoletta said emphatically. "Listen to me. I used to think I knew about love. Now I know that was just a child's dream. But since this has happened, I've found that my Guido *needs* me. That need is true love. Demetrio needs you. How can you go away and leave him all alone in that big house? Don't you know how lonely he's going to be?"

"I can't stay just to keep him company. It must be more than that. You say he needs me, but he'd die rather than say it."

"So? Because he's a fool, does that mean you have to be a fool, as well?"

Reva looked at her tenderly. Nicoletta's triumphant love made her think love could solve all problems. If only it could be so easy, she thought. "Demetrio doesn't trust me," she said. "He knows I was the photographer who worked on that article, and he thinks I was trying to sabotage everything. But I didn't know who owned those apartments, Nicoletta, honestly I didn't. It was just unlucky timing."

"Of course," Nicoletta said at once, as though the matter were too unimportant for comment. "I know you're not deceitful, and in his heart Demetrio knows it, too. Oh, Reva, something must happen to bring you two back together. It casts a shadow over my wedding to think that you two will part."

"Well, I suppose we can't all be like you and Guido. Be happy with him, Nicoletta, and don't worry about us. Demetrio doesn't really need me. He has all he wants."

On the night before her wedding, Nicoletta slipped into the room Demetrio used as an office in the house and put her arms about his neck. "I've come to say goodbye," she said softly. "There'll be no time to say it properly tomorrow."

"You're right," he said, embracing her warmly.

"And I want to say thank you. I was afraid you'd forbid me to marry Guido since I'm underage."

"You can thank Reva that I didn't. I made a mistake with her that I'll pay for all my life. I didn't want to make you hate me, too."

"But she doesn't hate you," Nicoletta said earnestly.

"She used to. Now she's just indifferent. She's only waiting for tomorrow to be over. Then she'll leave here and return to her true life."

"Her true life is with you," Nicoletta told him.

"She doesn't think so. If I believed—" Demetrio stopped.

"Yes?" Nicoletta said encouragingly.

He sighed. "Nothing. Everything has been said. Let her go back to England. There she has all she wants."

The sun shone on the little village church. The bride was given away by her brother, with her sister-in-law in attendance. The groom brought only his mother and a friend. His father refused to be present.

Reva's eyes stung as she watched Guido and Nicoletta give themselves to each other with whole hearts. That was the only kind of love that counted. It was a kind she'd been unable to win from Demetrio, and would never want from any other man.

After a small reception, Demetrio drove them to the airport. There were hugs all around. Reva tried not to meet Nicoletta's eyes. She was afraid of the beseeching question she would see in them. If only this could be over soon.

The last call came over the loudspeaker. "You'd better go now," Demetrio said, in a suspiciously husky voice.

Guido began to draw his wife away. She cast a last look back at her brother, then at Reva. Tears shone in her eyes. At the very last moment she cried out, "You are fools, both of you. *Fools.*" Then she was gone.

They returned to the car in silence. Demetrio got behind the wheel, but didn't start the engine. He seemed caught in a dream. "We'd better get back," Reva said gently. "I still have some packing to do."

With an effort, Demetrio said, "Reva, have you thought about what you're doing?"

"I haven't thought about anything else," she said heavily.

"Perhaps Nicoletta's right, and we're fools. I think you've made a hasty decision. We should at least talk about it."

And then, he thought, *perhaps the words would break through the barriers of his pride and touch her heart.*

"Is there anything to say that we haven't already said?" she asked.

"In many ways, we've said too much. We've flung hurtful accusations at each other instead of discussing our situation calmly."

"You think calm discussion is going to help?"

"It's the one thing we've never really tried. I believe we have something—something that's worth preserving."

He might have been talking about assets in the board-room, she thought despairingly.

As if to confirm her view, the car phone rang. Deme-trio snatched it up. As he listened, his brow darkened. "Come into the office?" he said. "Now?"

Reva could hear his secretary's voice. "Signor Brus-chi is here. He says it's vital that he talk to you at once."

"Very well, I'll come."

He swung the car out of the parking lot and headed back to the city. Reva thought wryly that if she'd had any doubts about the rightness of returning to England, this was her answer. Even at the moment when he was ask-ing her to stay with him, business came first.

As he pulled up in front of the office Demetrio said, "Would you mind waiting in the car? I won't be long."

"I'm coming up," she said. "I need some water to take a couple of aspirin. I'll go home by taxi. Please don't cut your meeting short."

He scowled, but didn't argue. When they reached his floor, he instructed his secretary to fetch her a drink and strode straight into the office. Through the open door, Reva saw a fat man rise and face him. There was just a moment when she was visible to the stranger, and she had the strangest feeling that he was taken aback. Then the door closed.

She sipped her mineral water and took some aspirins against the headache that was threatening her. She felt horribly tired. For a moment at the airport she'd had a brief flicker of hope, but it had died at once. There had been no passion in Demetrio's voice, and keeping her meant less to him than that meeting in there.

The secretary was on the phone again, sounding agitated. "Is something wrong?" Reva asked when she hung up.

"Yes. Someone on the third floor has— Oh, it's no use, I've got to go and sort it out myself." She indicated the door. "If he asks for me..."

"I'll tell him you've gone to sort out a crisis," Reva promised.

The secretary thanked her and hurried away. Reva felt it was time she called for a taxi, and she picked up the phone. But there was only silence from the other end. She hesitated over the bank of switches in front of her before flipping one she hoped would give her an outside line.

Then she nearly dropped the phone, for a voice had come from the intercom. Realizing that she'd inadvertently switched it on, she put down the phone and reached out to turn off the intercom, but she was stopped by the same voice speaking the name Alicia in tones of fear and loathing. "She's a threat to all of us," said the voice, one that Reva didn't recognize. "And to discover that you of all people are married to her..."

"We've been over this ground before." That was Demetrio.

"Yes, and I thought you understood the need to be rid of her."

Demetrio broke in on him. "Be very careful what you say, Bruschi. You're talking about my wife."

"But for how much longer? That's the point."

"Forever, if I can persuade her," Demetrio said simply.

Bruschi exploded. "Damn it, man, can't you see how she's damaging you? Since the apartment-block story, millions have been wiped off your shares. And why? Because nobody wants to risk contact with a man whose wife is spying on his associates to expose their little lapses.''

Demetrio's voice was deadly. "Don't ever dare speak of my wife like that again if you value your safety. She's no spy. She had no idea that Torvini was the culprit.''

"You're very naive if you believe that.''

"I've been called many things, Bruschi, but never naive. I know who's honest, and who isn't, and my wife is the most honest person alive. She's a person of courage and principle, and that's more than can be said of the men who've stampeded to desert me.''

"Well, if you really mean to allow her to stay—''

"You misunderstand," Demetrio said harshly. "I'm not going to *allow* her to stay. I'm going to beg and implore her to stay. Does that make my position clear?''

"Perfectly. I think you're completely mad—''

"I'm not mad. I've just come to my senses. Don't let me keep you.''

Reva didn't hear the last five words. She was standing there, fighting back tears. The discovery that she was ruining Demetrio's business, the work of his whole life, had hit her like a blow. She wondered how she could have been so stupid and self-absorbed as not to think of that. But she'd heard something that filled her with wonder— Demetrio defending her with a generosity that made her eyes sting and a lump come to her throat. This was the understanding she'd always longed for, but it had been bought at a terrible price to him.

She brushed a hand hastily across her eyes as the office door opened, but she wasn't fast enough. Bruschi marched out and stood glaring at her. "I hope you realize the damage you'll do him by staying here, *signora*," he barked, and he departed without giving her a chance to answer.

Demetrio's sharp eyes observed the position of the intercom button. "How much did you hear?" he asked quickly.

"Enough to know I'm ruining you," Reva said in despair.

"You're not ruining me. I'll ride out this storm."

"Suppose you don't. He said that millions had been wiped off your shares. Oh, how could I have been so stupid and selfish? Why didn't you tell me what was happening?"

"Tell you what? That a few fools are running scared because my wife is dedicated to the truth? Why should I worry you with such nonsense?"

"But it isn't nonsense. It's a threat to your life's work."

"No," he said simply, and with a note in his voice that she'd never heard before. "It's only a threat to my business, and no man should make business his life's work. My life's work is going to be...something else."

"But I'll never forgive myself for doing this to you."

He looked at her strangely. "Are you saying you'd stop exposing crooks and defending little people for my sake?" he asked.

Her hands flew to her mouth at hearing the dilemma stated so bluntly. "Perhaps I— Perhaps there might be a way that—" It was no good. The truth was staring her in the face, and her honesty couldn't shirk it. But Demetrio's eyes were filled with understanding, as though he were urging her to say the one crucial word. *"No,"* she whispered at last. "I can't."

"Thank God!" he said fervently. "Thank God I haven't made you less than yourself. I couldn't have borne that. I'll survive anything they can do to me. I may have to contract the company drastically, but it'll rise again. I'll sell the villa if I have to. I'll rather enjoy fighting my way up again. Climbing the ladder was always more fun than being at the top. But even if I thought I'd never get to the top again..." He looked at her, and there was something new in his face, something that made her pulse race in a way that was different from the sexual arousal he could inspire so easily. This was a turmoil of the heart.

"Even if I thought it would cost me everything I've worked for," he said deliberately, "I would still beg and implore you to stay with me, for I need you very much. I need your spirit of courage and decency. I need your impatience with deceit, your defiance, and your healthy, cleansing anger. But most of all, I need your love."

Reva stood watching him, transfixed, hardly able to believe that she was hearing the words she'd longed for. But this was a new Demetrio, saying incredible things.

"Nicoletta said we were both fools," he added, "and I've been a fool from the start. When I tricked you into returning to Milan, I was determined to use the situation as a way of getting you back. But I thought I could do it without sacrificing my pride and letting you see how desperately I need you. That's how great a fool I was. Love has no pride. If I'd learned that before—"

He got no further. Reva was in his arms, her mouth on his, trying to tell him through her kiss that she, too, had learned, and had been reborn in love. "Don't say any more," she begged when she could speak. "I was wrong too... so wrong..."

"Not as wrong as I," he said quickly. "Tell me that the past can be forgiven...."

"I'll forgive you if you'll forgive me."

"I tried to ask you to return to me at the airport, but I couldn't get the right words out. But when that man slandered you, I suddenly discovered the words. Let them do their worst. As long as we stand together, we're invincible.''

"Together," she said longingly. It had a beautiful sound.

She rested her head contentedly against him. Then a new thought came to her. "If you sell the villa, can you manage to keep your mother's cottage?"

"Yes, I'm determined on that. And about the cottage—there's something I have to tell you. It'll make you laugh at me, but I don't care."

"Tell me," she said, smiling to herself.

"Later. Tonight, when we're lying in each other's arms, that will be the time for secrets. Why are you smiling?"

"Because I, too, have a secret to tell you about the cottage. But it can wait. We have all the years ahead."

"Come home with me, my darling," he said softly. "It's time we began our marriage."

* * * * *

A romantic collection that
will touch your heart....

Diana Palmer
Debbie Macomber
Judith Duncan

As part of your annual tribute to
motherhood, join three of Silhouette's
best-loved authors as they celebrate the
joy of one of our most precious gifts—
mothers.

Available in May at your favorite retail outlet.

Only from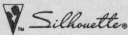

—where passion lives.

SMD93

INTIMATE MOMENTS®

10TH Anniversary

Celebrate our anniversary with a fabulous collection of firsts....

The first Intimate Moments titles written by three of your favorite authors:

NIGHT MOVES   Heather Graham Pozzessere
LADY OF THE NIGHT   Emilie Richards
A STRANGER'S SMILE   Kathleen Korbel

Silhouette Intimate Moments is proud to present a FREE hardbound collection of our authors' firsts—titles that you will treasure in the years to come from some of the line's founding members.

This collection will not be sold in retail stores and is available only through this exclusive offer. Look for details in Silhouette Intimate Moments titles available in retail stores in May, June and July.

SIMANN

SILHOUETTE® Desire®

HAWK'S WAY

HAWK'S WAY—where the Whitelaws of Texas run free till passion brands their hearts. A hot new series from Joan Johnston!

Look for the first of a long line of Texan adventures, beginning in April with THE RANCHER AND THE RUNAWAY BRIDE (D #779), as Tate Whitelaw battles her bossy brothers—and a sexy rancher.

Next, in May, Faron Whitelaw meets his match in THE COWBOY AND THE PRINCESS (D #785).

Finally, in June, Garth Whitelaw shows you just how hot the summer can get in THE WRANGLER AND THE RICH GIRL (D #791).

Join the Whitelaws as they saunter about HAWK'S WAY looking for their perfect mates . . . only from Silhouette Desire!